A Chess Master

A CHESS MASTER

Juhani Seppovaara

Gallinarium

The Finnish original: *Shakkimestari*, 2024
© Juhani Seppovaara and Docendo 2024

© 2025 Juhani Seppovaara, Gallinarium
Gallinarium, gallinarium20@gmail.com
www.juhaniseppovaara.fi

Translated by Timothy Binham

Graphic design, cover and layout by Minna Luoma
www.candygraphics.fi

Published by: BoD · Books on Demand, Mannerheimintie 12 B, 00100 Helsinki, bod@bod.fi

Printed by: Libri Plureos GmbH, Friedensallee 273, 22763 Hampuri, Saksa

ISBN: 978-952-80-9545-3

Years ago, I imagined how my life would end, heralded by a premonition as with the monks of old. I go back once more to the island where I spent my childhood holidays. I sit on the rocky shore, watching the shimmering, eternal sea. I get up and chop some firewood for heating the sauna. The thickest log is so knotty that I am unable to split it. I use a metal wedge, but it gets stuck. I strike again and again, dripping with sweat, until my eyes grow dim and I am gasping for breath. Finally I hear the final crunch as the log gives way, my last flash of consciousness in this world.

The end will come some other way. I realize planning it is not in my power.

A mole had appeared on my back; I spotted it by chance in a fitting room mirror. It resembled the forewing of a dead-nettle beetle, glittering in the colours of the rainbow. I willed it to rise up on its wings, but it did not.

A dermatologist removed the mole and sent it off to be diagnosed. It turned out to be a melanoma, although it was not clear whether it had metastasized. A larger tissue sample was then removed.

I had no symptoms, aside from occasional bouts of helplessness and anxiety. Nothing new there, however. Calm down, I told myself. To no avail. The wait for the results deprived me of sleep, and I sank into apathy, barely coping with my daily chores.

I was referred to follow-up examinations. A little later, I saw an oncologist. She patted my shoulder and said I had an aggressive type of cancer, with metastatic tumours that had spread via the lymph system all over my body.

I crumpled up in my chair, speechless. In that instant I realized my life had taken a new turn.

I had previously worried about diseases I might contract, although I knew my fear might increase the risk. Now it seemed as if providence was mocking me: my concern had not been unwarranted.

Surgery was possible, but apparently the risk of recurrence was particularly high in my case. Advanced melanoma is incurable; all that can be done is to slow down the advance of the disease and alleviate the symptoms with medication.

I did not dare ask how much time I had left. Neither did I have any desire to find out how the disease would progress, let alone when painful symptoms would set in and when my mind would start to disintegrate. I decided to follow the example of humankind by approaching the precipice back first.

I staggered out into the rush-hour roar. People were returning home from their day's business. Somewhere in the distance, an ambulance siren howled. Everything was as before, although nothing was the same. A strange feeling.

The shadows of icicles glittering in the eaves showed up in sharp contrast against the pale wall, dripping slowly. Soon the icicles will collapse. The polar ice caps, too, will melt. My tumours will remain.

Instead of returning home, I wandered like a sleepwalker through Berlin's Prenzlauer Berg, along streets to which I had become attached. There was no reason to do so, but neither was there any reason not to do so.

Dusk began to fall. I plunked myself down on the terrace of

the Café Al Hamra, my regular haunt, picked up a blanket from the back of a chair, and wrapped it around my body. As usual, the waiter brought me a cappuccino without asking. She sensed my dejection and looked confused, but I said nothing.

If my friend Daniel had happened to come by, I would have been glad to play a game of chess. It would have given me something else to think about, a chance to shut off all other thoughts. I leafed through the *Berliner Zeitung* until I realized I had not retained anything that I had read.

One would like ageing to be a merciful time, meekly accepting the inevitable ebb of the river of life. But my illness had interrupted its normal course. Nothing could be done to stop its meanders. I had no faith in miracle cures. I realized how fragile life is when fate pointed its finger at me. Its decree could not be appealed.

The departure of my closest friend Ilpo had already prepared me for the idea of the end. I had been sitting on a park bench on Helmholtzplatz when my phone beeped. A text from Ilpo's former wife appeared on the screen: Ilpo had been found dead in his bed.

The message, in black letters on a grey background, blurred before my eyes. I had trouble understanding what it said. Later that evening, I deleted Ilpo's contact information, setting the final seal on his departure.

I used to think there is a purpose to everything, including suffering, and to believe that adversity might be an augur of better things to come. But what purpose is served by a deadly disease?

A child does not have to learn to be happy; even a fool can enjoy happiness as an adult. Perhaps that is what created the need to embrace suffering. One has to learn to accept life's inherent tragedy.

In one of the classic Russian novels, a dying man praises the joys of life. Reading the book, it struck me that this was not an observation someone who had succeeded in everything would make.

Joseph Brodsky wrote that he had felt solidarity with grief alone, but until his mouth was stuffed with clay, it would utter words of gratitude.

In Dostoevsky's novel *The Idiot*, a priest arrives at the scaffold without the eucharist. The condemned men ask him why they have been deprived of their right to the last confession and absolution. They are told that they have been pardoned. They take this as an insult; they had mustered all their courage to meet death with dignity, all in vain.

If I were to be told now that the hospital had mixed up my x-rays with someone else's and that my cancer had not metastasized, I would not feel insulted, let alone disappointed.

Art depends on despair and death, and flirts romantically with them. If this were not so, no such words would ever be written, no statues would be sculpted and no symphonies composed. The shelves of libraries sag under the weight of murders. Literature abounds with contradictory ideas about how to live with death lurking behind one's back. Someone said I'm not afraid of dying, I just don't want to be there when it happens.

It was reassuring to speak of sinking into an eternal sleep or shuffling off this mortal coil. In wars, the victims of bombings die, but heroes fall. People who die on the home front never earn the nimbus of a hero even if they have acted more altruistically than front-line soldiers. Death is a spectrum that reflects the many shades of life.

It is not likely that I can avoid self-pity, but I hope that it will not turn into bitterness. I do not wish to leave this life with fists clenched. Cynicism never saved anyone.

I realized the importance of basic security and the happiness brought by a stable everyday life when they ceased to exist. How should I use the time left to me? Whom should I tell about my illness, and how? Should I pretend to be strong and try to console my confidant, even as black misery gnawed at my mind?

I spooned up the rest of the whipped cream from my cup and licked the spoon clean. The waiter brought glasses of white wine to the neighbouring table and asked me if all was well. I nodded and thought that's the only thing you could influence.

My next-door neighbour Marie appeared at my table. She pointed with her stick at the couple sipping white wine and said that we had also been young and beautiful once upon a time. I asked her if she missed those days. She smiled wanly and walked on.

Marie had once invited me to her flat for coffee and told me the story of her life. One morning in February 1942, her mother was arrested, and Marie had to go with her. The playground that she could see from her window was an *Umschlagplatz*, a collection point. A lorry crammed with the last Jews in the neighbourhood was waiting for them there.

At the gate to Birkenau concentration camp, Marie and her mother were dragged apart. They expected to be reunited later that day. Marie never heard from her mother again. Her father, a *Wehrmacht* officer, had been shot in Cracow one year earlier when he refused to execute a group of Polish officers taken as prisoners.

From Birkenau, Marie was taken to an educational institution for children at Sachsenhausen concentration camp. There she was trained as a nurse. After the war, she worked at the radiology department of Berlin-Buch Hospital. Following reunification, she was among the first batch of staff to be made redundant when Charité Hospital took over Berlin-Buch, which it saw as a rival. According to Marie, the age of the dictatorship of money had begun.

The red star in front of Al Hamra lit up. Returning home in the evenings, I could see it shining from a long way off. It made me feel at home. I could also see it from the windows of my flat. I had recently become aware that there was no birch tree in front of my house. Since a self-respecting Finn must have one, I had dug up a birch seedling in the forest and planted it in a metal bucket on my balcony.

I had built up a fine circle of friends in Berlin. Meanwhile, my ties with Finland had weakened, and my contacts with family and friends there had petered off. Now was my last opportunity to fix things. I also had inheritance issues and other practical arrangements to sort out. The mere thought made my forehead break out in a cold sweat.

There were many metres of literary masterpieces on my bookshelf. Many of these I would probably never re-read, even if I had enough years left to do so, but they still showed where my thoughts had wandered over the years. They would keep gathering dust even when I myself had turned into an urnful of ashes.

For sentimental reasons, I had brought to Berlin the collected works of Goethe inherited from my great-grandfather. I knew I would not read them, if only because the *Fraktur* type was so hard to read. Some of my more militant fellow students kept the collected works of Lenin on their bookshelves. A few even pretended to have read them.

Goethe's last words are said to have been *Mehr Licht*, More light! Perhaps he saw, or hoped to see, a flash of light. Now I began to suspect that what he actually said was *Mehr nicht*, Nothing more. Chekhov is supposed to have said *Ich sterbe*, I'm dying. If my original intention were to come true, I could cry out: "And yet it splits!".

There was no trusting all these last words. They were often held to embody some crystallized wisdom that the speaker had never intended, even if he had spoken the words.

I began to take an interest in Sicily when I read that Goethe said that if you have not seen Sicily, you have not really seen Italy. When going to Sicily, he intended to visit Syracuse, but never did so. I went there in his stead. Gazing at the shimmering Mediterranean from the terrace of a Baroque villa, I thought I could spend the twilight of my life there if something dramatic were to happen.

Perhaps a trip abroad might ease my distress now: no matter where to, but preferably somewhere near the sea. As a child, I had been given a globe. Spinning it, I immediately rejected all faraway lands. The globe showed the German Democratic Republic, a country to which no one can travel anymore.

On the Interrail trips of my youth, I gorged myself on new cities. In later years, I returned to those that brought back warm memories, highlights of my life. Now, however, my fond recollections of Paris or Prague might pale or turn painful if I went there. Perhaps my existence and its looming end could be viewed with fresh, untainted eyes in some place with which I had no ties.

I had drifted to East Berlin by chance. Now I paced back and forth in my flat and wondered what would happen to my cult artefacts from the GDR period and my large compass flag. They chronicled a turning point in my life. In the eyes of my heirs, they would probably be entertaining relics of a defunct state.

The clink of two light metal ice cream bowls against each other produced a bright sound. If you had never experienced it firsthand, it was just background noise. For my East Berlin friend Leo, a serving of pink yoghurt in a bowl like this brought back his childhood.

In early 1989, the beloved comrade Erich Honecker vowed that the Wall would stand for at least another hundred years. Even he must have realized that there is no Eternal City for us down here.

I had booked an appointment with my dentist for an implant after an infected tooth had had to be removed. I cancelled the appointment, as well as another appointment with a urologist. Even if I were to develop prostate cancer on top of everything else, I would not have time to die of it.

I could not postpone or forget everything, however. Death cleaning. The mere words brought a stab of pain. There were some horrors I would be spared. The ecosystem was about to collapse, but I would be gone before it happened. Perhaps living on the brink of disaster was a precondition for human life. I now looked at people, even young people, with this thought at the back of my mind.

I had shoeboxes full of photographs taken by my father and grandfather to sort. They recounted the lives of my parents and forefathers in the form of a happy string of pearls interspersed with war, disease and disasters. There were also thousands of my own photographs to catalogue and slides to scan. This task would enable me to relive my own years and the chain of generations that I would soon be taking leave of. But did I really wish to relive them?

In older years, I had come to think that life was too valuable to devote to topical matters. Now I had lost all residual interest in them. I still watched football, but this was by way of escape. Every match might be the last I could watch untroubled by symptoms and with senses intact.

Out in the wide world, wars were being fought, villages were being drowned by floods, fields were being devastated by drought, children were dying of hunger and disease. None of these tragic facts could match my death sentence. It was my last thought when I went to sleep and my first thought when I woke up.

I had had a brush with death once before, when I found myself in the eye of a storm in a small sailing boat. I had to tear down the sails. The raging waves threatened to smash my boat against the rocks. When the storm finally died down, I felt as though no earthly worry could ever touch me again. That feeling lasted a few months.

The long grey season of another Berlin winter was over. Spring, though long-awaited, still came as a surprise in the year 2021 of our Lord. The blackbird's melodious flute chirped in the park on Helmholtzplatz. Purple crocuses rose from the dead. In Finland, this was the season of crusty spring snow that I missed in Berlin.

The scent of bird cherry blossom used to intoxicate me in spring. Now I was afraid it would plunge me into instant melancholy.

At Al Hamra, a drab-looking man solved crossword puzzles, day after day. He was killing time. Life is so short that he will probably never tire of his meaningless task. I envied him. He seemed to have detached himself from the passage of time, and the repetitiveness of his days hardly bothered him; perhaps, indeed, it was a source of satisfaction.

What point was there in passion anymore? Or in seizing the day? Banal actions like filing one's tax returns had been time-consuming chores. If only one could concentrate on them without the shadow of a cancer diagnosis, and detect the halo over a cast-iron frying pan, for example.

I slept poorly, and was exhausted during the day. I imagined that my fatigue was due to illness rather than sleeplessness. Whenever I had a headache, I feared that the disease had reached my brain.

Facebook sent me an advertisement for a Finnish birch coffin with tasselled corners. Perhaps the undertakers had made a deal with the oncologist. Deutsche Telekom sent me an e-mail offering a phone with an sos function. Someone wants what is best for you, right until the very end.

Before my diagnosis, I used to sit on the balcony, sipping classic Finnish vodka flavoured with my own plums, and thought I lacked for nothing. The flavour brought back memories of getting ready to go to a country dance. This sensation had freed me from the relentless yoke of time, producing an unthinking peace.

A plum tree grew by the cart path on the far shore of Lake Oberuckersee in Brandenburg. When I rowed back across the lake, drops of water glittered on the oars, and the squeaking oarlocks struck a childhood note. I thought of someone else rowing my boat when I would no longer be able to do so or would no longer be around.

Gusts of wind ruffled the lake surface, then the wind died down and the lake turned into a mirror of the sky. Deceits of lapwings were preparing to migrate. It was as though they were calling me to go south with them.

If you had to see some meaning in life, it was in moments like these. It was a good sign to have no need to seek such meaning. Useless speculation and the need to understand merely chipped away at the lyrical undercurrent of life. Aimlessness had induced some people to dream of a career as a philosopher, as if that could clarify anything. Wishing to see the world, I had rejected philosophy.

My serenity was gone. Since there was no escape from the end of the line, all I could do was confront and accept it. I tried to detect some unique lustre in my shrinking life. I had lived a long, good life, and was not far off from reaching the average lifespan. After a professional aberration, I had found a path to the source of my spiritual essence. In any case, the time to leave was drawing near.

The idea of eternal life was invented to ease the pain of life's brevity. According to an old Finnish saying, people live as long as they are remembered. It is a lovely thought, but can only console those who are left behind. My life seemed to be fading away before reaching maturity.

I did not believe in relief brought by hard drinking; it could only make matters worse. I went back to the books that had once meant so much to me. I could see words and sentences on the paper, but not the thoughts behind them.

I feared that I would collapse under the weight of my chaotic thoughts. In my plight, I fled to the logical, organized world of chess, hoping to banish my visions of terror to a hazy horizon. The progression of moves obeyed my will; in the maze of variations, clarity of thought was crucial, and there was no room for chance.

Sitting face to face and conversing with my opponents had once been a key feature of my fascination with chess, but now it seemed natural to play blitz on the internet. On the basis of previous games, the portal knew every player's level of skill, and picked an opponent of the same level in seconds. The opponent's name was accompanied by a country flag. Whenever I saw the Russian flag, this brought a particular electric jolt and a spirit of revenge to the game.

Chess provided a moment of oblivion from the world outside. I played endless series of games, only stopping when I became so tired that I began to make more and more losing blunders.

After moving to Berlin a decade ago, I used to sit at Al Hamra every day. The regular customers knew each other by name and shook hands when they met. Two men often played chess at a corner table. Once they caught me watching from the corner of my eye, and one of them challenged me to a game.

From that day, I used to play Daniel once a week. He had also learned the rules as a little boy. I trusted that the chess would not get out of hand, as it had when I was a child.

To begin with, Daniel played better, but I gradually attained the same level. My games with him were a duel between egos, an extension of our political debates. In chess, you could prove the superiority of your argument objectively.

I considered Daniel to be Putin's mouthpiece. Our political views were so far apart that our arguments were merely frustrating. When we spoke about universal issues, however, we understood each other very well. We also had a similar skewed sense of humour.

I felt an urgent need to beat Daniel again. My melanoma diagnosis led me to a manic study of historical chess masterpieces, from which I learned some ingenious variations. By any sensible measure, this was a complete waste of my dwindling time, but in my plight I was unable to think sensibly.

Daniel's father Rainer was involved in plotting the assassination of Hitler in 1943. He was caught, but the evidence was flimsy, and he got off with a two-year prison sentence.

Rainer was allowed to take with him a book containing some of the greatest games in chess history, but his chess set was taken from him. He hid slices of dark and white bread in his cell. When they dried, he used a pair of nail scissors to cut chess pieces out of them and a brick fragment to draw a chessboard on the floor.

He went over the games time and again, but realized that playing himself was a sure path to madness. One of the prison guards had a chess set in his booth. Rainer befriended him and persuaded him to play. The guard would make his move when he brought gruel and bread to the cell. On the next visit, Rainer would play his move, and so on. After the war, the two men happened to meet in a café and played one last game, which ended in a draw.

During the Cold War, Rainer was involved in setting up a network in West Berlin that searched for people arrested or missing in the Soviet zone and helped victims of persecution escape to the West. For the GDR leaders, he was a nightmare enemy. He thought it an irony of fate that if it had not been for Hitler, the GDR never would have existed, and the course of his life would have been completely different. Rainer later founded the Checkpoint Charlie Museum with CIA support.

When Rainer died, Daniel inherited his father's chess book. He studied the games in it and was often able to relate a position in our games to something he had learned from the book.

By the time I was eight years old, I had read to tatters the book *120 Short Masterpieces* by the Finnish chess master Eero Böök. Ever since then, leafing through that book has brought back childhood memories. In those days, life seemed endless.

I was particularly impressed by a game in which the former child prodigy Samuel Reshevsky had the temerity to play Alekhine's Defence against the world champion after whom this opening had been named. You can't always win, even at chess, but Reshevsky's audacity was enviable, and a dash of that swashbuckling attitude found its way into my playing style. I later hoped to emulate the same spirit in my lifestyle.

My engineer father stopped playing with me after he began to lose repeatedly. My grandfather, however, was not bothered by losing. He managed to avoid obvious errors, but his manoeuvres lacked a winning plan, and our games became monotonous. I learned from him that the Russian equivalent for bishop meant 'elephant', whereas the French word meant 'fool'. Whenever he threatened my Queen, he always said *garde!*, which was an old gentlemanly custom. He was the same age then as I am now.

I bought new chess books. I saw the chessboard grid pattern in Finnish crispbread, in the floor tiles at my school and in the Helsinki city map on the hallway wall at home. At school, I hid a thin volume of chess games between my schoolbooks.

At night I went over the games of masters in my mind for many wakeful hours. I had nightmares in which the pieces turned into demons and monsters. I could no longer distinguish between dream and reality. I was dead tired during the day.

After yet another sleepless night, I realized that I would have to give up chess. Soon I began to wake up well-rested in the mornings again. Crispbread became mere crispbread, made of God's grain. A horse's gentle gaze, hairy coat and warm breath stirred me more than a wooden knight on a chessboard. I tasted the joys of childhood again.

At the age of 17, I went to Minnesota as an exchange student, sailing on a ship called the *Seven Seas*. Onboard were seven hundred young people from all over Western Europe. A chess tournament in knockout format was arranged during the crossing. I made it to the semi-finals without any difficulty. There I played a Swedish opponent whom my fellow Finns considered to be a self-satisfied boor. My compatriots thought it was my patriotic duty to beat him, and I could not disappoint them. That game was more than just a game.

In the final, I faced a Dutch opponent who was known to be the youth champion of his country. I imagined that all I had to do was to avoid mistakes and follow well-proven strategies: I could not possibly lose.

A ring of spectators, including my previous opponents, gathered around the table, absorbed in the twists and turns of the game. This was a new experience for me, but I concentrated on the pieces and forgot my confusion. The situation was something like the game described in Stefan Zweig's *Chess Story*, played on a ship travelling from New York to Buenos Aires.

I soon became aware of my opponent's tactical superiority. He played flawlessly, and induced me to make errors. From one move to the next, my defences began to crumble, until finally my position was hopeless, and I tipped my king to resign.

My opponent was an amiable fellow, which made my loss easier to bear. His superior skill was not just a gift from God, however. I realized that if I wanted to achieve something in chess, I would have to devote my next years to it, without any guarantee of success. At any rate, my opponent was miles ahead of me. In the worst case, I might eventually feel that I had wasted years of my life.

Minnesota was an intellectual desert. At the beginning of my return journey, I felt like tying the Statue of Liberty to the ship's aft hook by the neck.

In many ways, that year was to shape the direction of my life. My American family's unwavering, stifling faith and theatrical piety had taxed my energy, and I leapt aside from that path. I thought damnation and salvation were just another form of intimidation and seduction used to control people. It was liberating to think that God neither exists nor does not exist. I became an atheist by the grace of God.

For many decades, I forgot about chess and only played occasionally, until I rediscovered the game in Berlin. The impetus came from a video clip in which Marcel Duchamp gave a poetic account of his own chess playing. He said chess was the part of his life he enjoyed most. It also provided him with a break from painting, making it possible for him to avoid repeating himself as an artist. He had started playing in his youth, and said he would keep playing until his dying day. He was said to need chess like a small child needs a nursing bottle.

Watching that clip once more, I saw it with new eyes. If Duchamp wanted to take chess with him to the land of shadows, why should not I? Better to be kept awake by chess than by thoughts of death.

Night after night, my computer screen kept flashing. I sifted through games played by legendary grandmasters over more than a century, and listened to analyses of them. Capablanca, Alekhine,

Botvinnik, Reshevsky, Smyslov, those household names from my childhood, along with the names of the opening variations they played, took on a magical resonance in my ears: the Spanish Four Knights' Game, the Dragon Variation of the Sicilian Defence, the King's Indian Attack. My imagination glided from one country to the next, and the chessboard kept the evil world outside far away.

In my ears, Capablanca became Casablanca, which only added to the name's lustre. I remember Capablanca writing that he only calculated one move ahead, but it was the correct one. The claim illustrated the great master's ego, but it could not possibly be true.

I saw myself as a child, moving the pieces in imitation of master games. I dreamed of a game in which I played myself at the age of eight. The present-day me would win, but only after a hard fight. Perhaps I would have warned myself of the dangers of excessive playing.

I also went over the games of the dramatic match between Bobby Fischer and Boris Spassky, which the Russian world champion lost. Played in Reykjavik in 1972, this match reflected the Cold War and measured the credibility of the two superpowers.

That same year I married and got a job with the Bank of Finland, the country's central bank. I built a house in Kirkkonummi, a rural community near Helsinki, cleared the alder thicket to make a garden, and built a chicken coop and an outdoor toilet at one end of the yard. All this was perhaps an instinctive attempt to capture something of the vanishing Finland of my childhood. Life was like the open sea, calling out to the sailor.

Late one evening, I chanced upon a photograph of a grey-haired man sitting on the lid of the seat in an accessible toilet and staring at the screen of a mobile phone. The photo was taken at an angle from above, evidently unbeknownst to the subject.

The accompanying caption said that the man in question was chess grandmaster Igors Rausis, and that the occasion was a tournament in Strasbourg in 2019. Rausis was the oldest grandmaster to be ranked among the top 100 players in the world at the time.

As soon as Rausis was shown the photo, he admitted to having used a computer chess application during the game. He withdrew from the tournament before he could be excluded. This marked a turning point in his life, and perhaps derailed it, or so I assumed. He was stripped of his grandmaster title and banned from competition for six years.

If you are a sprinter, in practical terms a ban like this spells an end to your career. By the time his ban expired, Rausis, too, probably would have been too old to play at the top level. Perhaps an experience like that would make you want to stop playing altogether.

The humiliating photo haunted me. I dreamed of Rausis as a wild animal in a cage, awaiting slaughter, with nowhere to hide from the spectators' gaze. In a vision generated by my excessive playing as a child, a rampant horse threatened to trample me under hoof.

Why did Rausis act as he did? Did he hope to improve his rating (a number indicating his relative status in the chess hierarchy) as his career was beginning to draw to a close? He must have realized that this might result in an ignominious end to a distinguished career. And was the insolent photographer ever charged with his crime?

An internet article revealed the broad facts of Rausis's life. Born in the Ukrainian province of Lugansk in the Soviet Union in 1961, he had grown up in Sevastopol. He had studied medicine, but had only worked in the profession for a few years. He was said to be seriously ill.

Throughout his adult life, Rausis had played and taught chess in various countries. He had gained the grandmaster title in 1992 and won the Latvian Championship in 1995. He had been living in Riga since 1984. Soon after moving to Latvia, he had enrolled in an elite academy in Moscow to study chess coaching.

I could not find any reference to what Rausis had been doing after the Strasbourg tournament. Had he made his last moves there? Had he also lost his self-respect? Was he even still alive? Could it be that the shame of the abrupt end to his career had resulted in his collapse?

Presumably he had been using an accessible toilet because of his illness. I found the very phrase 'accessible toilet' jarring. Would I be obliged to use one myself?

The photograph did not show any visible disability. He might have thought that the risk of getting caught in an accessible toilet was minimal. Had he already been cheating before he was caught? According to the article, there had been rumours.

In 2006, I had read about the 'toiletgate' controversy surrounding the world championship match between incumbent world champion Veselin Topalov and grandmaster Vladimir Kramnik. Topalov's manager complained to the organizers about Kramnik's repeated visits to the toilet, and suggested that Kramnik had received computer assistance there. The episode was dismissed as psychological warfare by Topalov's team in a hard-fought match. No evidence of cheating was found.

If all the moves made by one of the two players turn out to be those recommended by a computer, the player may be found guilty of cheating, though this depends on whether they have played like a human being or like a computer. This kind of evidence is not conclusive, however. Grandmasters do not need the help of a computer for most of their moves, but at certain points in the game even one move may be decisive. By contrast, an amateur player will not get far with the help of just one brilliant move.

The inclination to cheat makes people inventive. Someone had taped a mobile phone to their leg and received assistance via a microscopic earphone. At all major tournaments, players were scanned for electronics. As Lenin taught, "trust is good, but control is better". Was this why Rausis had only been playing in minor tournaments as the only participating grandmaster for years before he was caught?

Investigating Rausis's fate became an obsession for me. I wanted to know if his cheating had been linked to his illness, whatever it was. What he had done was not strictly a crime, whereas photographing him in the toilet and publishing the result was. What had been the outcome, or had the issue been played down? One would imagine that FIDE, the international chess federation, had been aware of the consequences of publishing that photograph. Could its action be explained by its being on the Kremlin's leash?

A Finnish friend told me that Rausis had also played in a couple of tournaments in Finland. I contacted two Finnish top players who I assumed might have played in the same tournaments.

One of them had actually played against Rausis. He thought

Rausis an agreeable person and said he had felt sorry for him because of the events in Strasbourg. He had heard rumours that Rausis was ill, but did not know what had become of him after the tournament. The other player I interviewed said that Rausis had ruined the reputation of the royal game, and that he should therefore have been clapped in the stocks in Riga's Cathedral Square.

Neither of them had Rausis's contact details. I wrote to the spokesperson of the Latvian Chess Federation as well as to the managing director of FIDE, who was one of Latvia's strongest woman players and had studied in Finland. Neither of them answered my e-mails; perhaps Rausis had become *persona non grata*.

I was about to abandon my quest. However, thoughts of the horror of cancer came back to haunt me, and pondering Rausis's fate seemed to keep them at bay. Again and again, I imagined the situation in which he had been shown the photograph. It was like the smoking gun after the crime, the moment the culprit soiling the reputation of chess had finally been caught red-handed.

The only way to get to the bottom of the affair was to go to Riga to try and find Rausis. Someone there was bound to know where he lived or worked. There was nothing to keep me in Berlin, and I did not believe that everyday routines would dull my pain.

Riga would be the first new city of the rest of my life, and probably the last. I imagined that the journey would free me from the vicious circle of speculation and fend off the fear of death, which I knew was the root of all evil. I had nothing to lose.

It also occurred to me that if I found Rausis, and if he agreed to cooperate, I could write an article about his life, my last contribution to the world of literature and my farewell to chess. We were fellow sufferers, and he was a trained physician. Perhaps he could help me in my distress.

All that I knew about Riga was based on my grandfather's stories. In normal circumstances, that feeble link would not have sufficed to induce me to travel, but nothing was normal now.

I had tacked some old postcards to the cork noticeboard in my writer's den. One had been sent from Jurmala and showed the Majorenhoff sea pavilion. My grandfather had sent it to my mother during the last summer before the war. He had sailed with his brother from their island holiday home via Tallinn to Riga. In the card, he praised this shining pearl of the Baltic and the seaside resort life in Jurmala.

I had inherited my grandfather's travel diaries from my parents. One contained descriptions of Riga. I dug them out and planned to follow in his footsteps there. Apparently one of Riga's parks was famous for its chess players. Perhaps they would receive a tourist in their fold, and surely one of the players would know Rausis.

Since the Baltic Express rail connection from Warsaw to Tallinn no longer existed, the train trip from Berlin to Riga would last 24 hours. I browsed the web for flights to Riga and found a convenient one with Ryanair for the following week. It cost a third of what I had paid for a train trip from Berlin to Hamburg, where I had attended a tango festival. I booked a room for one week at the Hotel Monika.

I scrolled down the calendar on my phone. The future years flashed past, with no end in sight. By the time I got to the year 4000, I had had enough. The first day of that year will be Saturday – sauna evening for many Finns. The thought made me dizzy. Whoever needed all those centuries? Would cockroaches finally have inherited the earth by then?

As a little boy I used to play chess with my grandfather on the sauna veranda. He would gaze seaward and grieve that the Baltic countries had been stranded behind the Iron Curtain. All the way to the horizon, all we could see was open sea, and I could not understand what he was talking about. Looking out from the triangulation tower at the highest point of the island with a pair of binoculars, one might catch a glimpse of the towers in Tallinn's old town. It was a fairytale sight.

My brother had inherited my grandfather's small yacht, which we sailed to Tallinn to watch the sailing competitions of the Moscow Olympics. It was an exceptional opportunity, as normally crossing the Gulf of Finland in one's own boat was forbidden. A stiff side wind carried us across in just seven hours. We would have loved to continue to Riga after the races, but it was not permitted. By then, I knew what the Iron Curtain meant.

Before going to trip to Riga, I studied Rausis's games. He played in a clinically precise, classical style, avoiding risks. It was diametrically opposed to the style of Mikhail Tal, the Wizard of Riga, who often sacrificed material for positional compensation to confuse his opponent. Tal had a unique ability to judge when to sacrifice. As he said, "There are two types of sacrifices, correct ones and mine." It was also said that he hypnotized opponents with his intense stare.

Many of Rausis's games were short. Perhaps he proposed a draw at an early stage in order to save energy for the decisive games, or maybe his opponent did because Rausis was so difficult to beat. However, one of his games had lasted over two hundred moves.

Rausis had won a tournament in Jyväskylä a quarter of a century earlier. In his game against Finland's No. 1 player Jouni Yrjölä, Rausis opened cautiously, but later played a surprising winning move. This was a departure from his usual prudent style.

I packed a couple of changes of clothes in a rucksack I had purchased in Tallinn long ago with rubles exchanged on the black market. I crammed my passport, flight tickets and a few books in a leather shoulder bag. Its bottom corner gaped at the seams, but I had not bothered to have it repaired. I thought it would last for what remained of my journey.

On the plane, a hundred souls or so sat, belted to their seats. It was too late to wonder whether my trip made any sense. The man sitting next to me was reading a Russian newspaper. His bony fingers, stained yellow with tobacco, looked like chicken claws. He behaved like a Finn: he did not greet me when I sat down, nor did he even look at me once. Perhaps he suspected me of being a Russophobe fascist.

The safety announcement followed. The standard performance, with hardly anyone watching. Instructions on the location of the safety exits, how to use the oxygen mask and the life jacket. The flight attendant showed us how to take out the whistle in the life jacket. In what kind of situation would it be useful? When floating in our yellow life jackets in an icy sea that had just swallowed up our plane?

Eight emergency exits were marked in the diagram on the back of the seat. If there was smoke in the cabin, we were supposed to crawl towards one of them. If I saw that an engine was burning and the oxygen masks dropped from the ceiling panels, would my fear be any less acute than before I was diagnosed?

I could make out clusters of wind turbines below. I had heard that the turbine blades mutilated birds. That was the price to pay for being able to enjoy my beer chilled in summer.

I took out of my bag Garry Kasparov's book *How Life Imitates Chess*. Kasparov ruled the roost in the chess world for nearly twenty years. I thought that besides chess, life also imitates chicken poop: one side is white and the other black.

According to Kasparov, chess was put on earth to deaden boredom, sharpen the wits, and fortify the spirit. He borrowed this rather obvious idea from Zweig's *Chess Story*.

Kasparov writes that players must learn to recognise their strengths and weaknesses and to adapt their style of play accordingly. An aggressive style suited him. Pruning your weaknesses is the quickest way to make progress both in chess and in life in general. If you have no long-term objective, your moves become reactive, and you will find yourself playing your opponent's game rather than your own. That is what had happened to my grandfather in my games with him.

Even the best strategy may fail due to poor tactical execution or lack of self-confidence, says Kasparov. Chess is a battle of nerves between two wills. On the other hand, excessive self-confidence may backfire. In a tight spot, however, it may be worth pretending self-confidence, especially if you are innately insecure. I thought the same rule could be applied to boxing, for example.

When writing about the world of chess or about Putin's tyranny, Kasparov knows what he is talking about. In 2012, he was accused of biting a policeman at a protest rally against the Pussy Riot trial. The parallels he draws between chess and life, however, are clumsy and artificial. Being a genius in one category may generate an illusion of mastery in other walks of life.

I recalled that chess had been used in many films and novels to demonstrate the protagonist's intelligence and strategic thinking. Chess works as a metaphor for many things. There has always been cheating in chess, and fraud is a popular theme in art. Writers play tricks to make their fabrications appear true. They also like to depict other fraudsters. Some crooks have flaunted their chess skills in order to gain other people's trust.

Perhaps I should have taken some other book with me; something by Chekhov, for instance. I used to re-read Chekhov's short stories every few years. Even a child enjoys stories being repeated. Chekhov's short stories are timeless, and provide a more precise and comprehensible account of human beings and society than all the academic twaddle produced in the fields of psychology, sociology and philosophy. Einstein once said that he learned more from Dostoevsky than from any scientist.

This time around, however, I would have steered clear of Chekhov's studies of disillusionment. *A Dreary Story* tells the tale of an old, infirm professor whose life becomes devoid of meaning. The mood is one of pervasive sadness. There is no catharsis at the end. Perhaps this story reflected Chekhov's own life, overshadowed by tuberculosis.

Down below, the sea ebbed and flowed. A flight attendant announced that we were approaching Riga. I marked my place in the book with a rooster feather and took out my passport. This was likely to be my last passport. Usually, we do not know which will be the last one, which is just as well. I hoped that I would not begin to resemble my passport photo towards the end.

Taxis swarmed around the airport exit, and I stepped into the closest one. The smell of tobacco and stale booze inside was too strong to be dispelled by the star-spangled Wunderbaum hanging from the rear-view mirror. I asked the driver whether the name Igors Rausis rang a bell. He knew that Rausis was a chess player, but that was all.

We advanced in fits and starts. Someone honked their horn, but it did not make the traffic move any faster. In the dream sequence in Federico Fellini's film *8 1/2*, the protagonist's car is caught in a traffic jam. Frustrated, he climbs out of the door and rises up into the air.

As far as I was concerned, cars were an invention of the devil. Apart from all the other evil they have caused, they have drowned out the original sounds of the city. On a visit to Paris long ago, wandering through the streets long after midnight, I could hear pigeons grunting, waves splashing in the Seine, and the leaves of trees rustling in the wind. Somewhere in the distance, a barge horn tooted. On my walks around Helsinki in the white summer nights of my youth, the only sounds were seagulls' cries and swifts' screeches.

The driver sighed and drummed the steering wheel. I understood from his swearing that the traffic jam had been caused by an accident. He spoke a little Russian and English, but both of us realized that we would only be able to communicate in awkward half-sentences.

Once in Berlin, I happened to get the same taxi driver twice. She remembered me the second time and told me she had kicked out her husband. She had tolerated her husband's macho ways when she was still young and in love. Now she was no longer either. Her father-in-law was even worse: he spent his evenings watching TV soaps and Turkish football matches, with an ancient, scruffy shepherd's hat on his head.

It still had not dawned on her husband that their son liked boys. That would be the day. This was the final straw that made her decide to divorce him.

Her husband had stolen her youth. Now she feared that no one would find her desirable anymore. When we arrived at my destination, she wondered where to find a decent man, opened the side window and lit a cigarette.

As we approached the city centre, the traffic gradually started moving again. The parks were bathed in the oblique sunlight of evening. I recognised the Freedom Monument as it flashed by, but I did not know what kind of freedom it had originally been meant to honour. Freedom and democracy are words that can mean anything and nothing. In the "people's democratic republic" of Latvia, the people had been deprived of both freedom and democracy.

The yawning hotel receptionist had never heard of Rausis. I filled in my check-in form in block letters, lugged my belongings up to the room and opened the window, which looked out on a courtyard. There was nothing in the room to indicate what part of the world I was in. There was no local beer in the fridge, no copy of a landscape painting by a Latvian artist in the room. We were living in a united Europe.

I threw myself down on the bed, trying to think about nothing.

Think I did nonetheless, although it seemed as though I had already thought every thought. These musings did nothing to dispel my gloom. My reclining position seemed like preparation for what was to come.

The silence was oppressive. It would not have bothered me to hear a couple quarrelling or making love next door. I should have booked a room on the street side.

The ceiling light was shaped like a shallow soup bowl. Squinting up at it, the light fixture turned into a flying saucer. Why was I staring at the ceiling in a strange city where I did not know another soul?

I fled from these gloomy thoughts to the hotel restaurant, where I ordered prawn pasta and a glass of red wine. I pondered the series of coincidences that had brought me here. On the wall, I spotted a German sentence which translates as "I know that I know nothing, but I seek the truth." A fine line, perhaps derived from Socrates.

The truth was not what I was seeking, however; I was looking for Rausis. What if I failed to find him? Even if I did manage to find him, he might not want to discuss his chess career and its ignominious end. In that case, a week in Venice, or perhaps in Goethe's footsteps in Naples, would have served me better. The dreamlike splendour of Venice might have emphasized how close the end was, eradicating the last shreds of joy in my life.

Back in my room, I checked my e-mail. It was all junk. I got into bed and read a few pages of Kasparov's book. His musings about society were an effective soporific.

After a restless night, I woke up from a dream in which I was playing a chess tournament. In my first-round game, I realized I had forgotten the rules for castling. To my embarrassment, I had to ask my opponent. He replied sarcastically "Does it matter anymore?", and guffawed.

I was afraid that soon I would not remember how the pieces moved even when I was awake. As my eyes wandered around the room, I did not understand where I was. My blanket and sheets were all heaped up at the foot of the bed. For a moment, I felt relief. Everything was all right, until I realized that it was not. Perhaps waking from a happy dream would have been even more painful.

Before the trip, I had read about a chess player who drove his opponent to distraction by humming the song *I'll Be Around When You're Gone* over and over again, reaching for the pieces as if he intended to make a move. Perhaps that was the source of my dream.

On the table, there was an empty beer can, my iPad, my passport and a few odd sheets of paper. A diagram showing the emergency exits, *evakuācijas plans*, hung on the wall. Sunlight filtered through a crack between the curtains, tracing a bright rhomboid figure on the mouse-grey carpeting. The figure shifted slowly, marking the passage of time, but that was not the purpose of its movement.

I took a cold shower, even though hot water was available these days. I opened the window and let the cool draught of air dry my body. The hotel walls framed a shaft leading down to a courtyard with waste containers gleaming in the light of the morning sun. It reminded me of the closed courtyards in the Helsinki of my childhood, where the only sign of life was dandelions pushing through cracks in the pavement. In the winter, the caretaker would make a skating rink for the children, until eventually cars took over the whole yard.

I read on my iPad that Finnish hockey players had done well in last night's NHL games. Outside the arenas, the heat had been scorching.

'Ellie' had sent me an e-mail saying: "Hi! Holding you between my legs in a vise. That's where I want to see you, your face gazing up into my eyes while I tremble all over and my pussy's still quivering after you've snuffed out its fire, then lit it again with your tongue. You will, won't you?"

My Mexican friend Maria, who lived in Berlin, wrote that her father was going blind. His loss of sight could be slowed down with eye drops, but it could not be stopped. Her father had said he did not want to live anymore once the world had gone dark. Maria was distressed and felt powerless in the face of her father's approaching death.

Maria was an artist, and the key element in her work was light. Even so, she had tried to comfort her father by saying that he could make up for the loss of his eyesight with his other senses. He was not convinced.

I was at a loss for words to comfort her. I had not told her about my own illness yet. Nor did I know how I would want to be comforted, or whether I would want to be comforted at all.

After breakfast, I went to Vērmanes Park, which the hotel receptionist said was the traditional place to go for chess buffs. Urban bustle gave way in the park to spring greenery and floral splendour. A poster next to an open-air stage advertised the International Mask Festival. When I worked as an economist at Finland's central bank, the mask of efficiency threatened to fuse with the skin on my face.

I asked a woman reading a book where to find the chess players. She said they would arrive after noon and sit on the benches next to the stage. She also told me that there was a monument to world champion Mikhail Tal at the other end of the park. She had once seen an old man weeping in front of it.

I found the bust of Tal and took a photograph. Not a dazzling work of art, but it did show how much the Latvians appreciate chess. I wish I had seen Tal playing in the park. In Narva, I had photographed the bronze statue of another chess legend, the Estonian grandmaster Paul Keres, sitting in front of a chessboard and gazing into the distance. The chair opposite was empty. The board showed a position from his last game. I sat down to determine what move I would have played against Keres. I did not bother to check my computer for the best move.

It is said of Keres that he never became world champion because he lacked the killer instinct. He died of a heart attack in Helsinki on his way home from a tournament in Vancouver. Reportedly he used to caress the pieces gently, as he might have caressed a woman's cheek. The pieces had had pleasant associations for him ever since he was a child. My experience was similar.

World champion Vassily Smyslov is said to have moved the pieces as if he wanted to screw them into the board. Such mannerisms reflect a player's personality. Smyslov was a boxer in his youth, which may have been reflected in his pugnacious attitude.

In a second-hand bookshop in Tallinn, I once bought a five-crown note issued by the Bank of Estonia and featuring a portrait of Keres. The underside showed a landscape from his native city Narva. Returning from a trip to Cuba, my chess partner Daniel brought me a one-peso coin bearing the image of world champion José Raúl Capablanca making a move. Chess is said to have been Capablanca's mother tongue.

I walked along Freedom Street towards the towering Freedom Monument. During the war, this street briefly bore the name Adolf-Hitler-Strasse; after the war it became Lenin Street, until eventually the original name was reinstated.

Apparently the Freedom Monument was called "the Travel Agency" during the Soviet period. Anyone who laid flowers before it received a free one-way ticket to Siberia.

A narrow stream ran through the verdant Kronvalds Park. The water sparkled blindingly in the sun. The iron railing of the arched bridge was full of love locks, symbols of undying love. In Paris, the combined weight of these love tokens once made a bridge railing collapse.

The sanded footpaths were flanked by wide pansy and tulip borders. I had read that flowers were particularly important to the Latvians. A woman in an orange vest crouched by the side of the path, weeding the flower beds. Latvia was no longer obliged to weed out dissidents.

The trees had attained a shade of bright green. All of creation breathed bright, blossoming May. Some writer asked the leading question: How should there be spring without death? For me, this could have been a moment of happiness untainted by the thought of cancer.

Clusters of Turkish rocket grew on the riverbanks, the same plant that could be seen in the early summer on the battlements of Suomenlinna, an island fortress off Helsinki. The seeds originally arrived in fodder fed to soldiers' horses, during a time when Finland was under Russian rule. The following words had been carved in Russian in the rocks by the shore: "Engraved by the hapless prisoner Ivan Vodopyanov on the 26th day of October 1830." Perhaps Ivan, gazing out to the open sea, had suddenly become aware of life's finitude, inducing him to record a lasting message in the rock.

"Vodopyanov" means someone who gets drunk on water. That was a form of inebriation that I had recommended to a number of friends who were teetering on the brink of the abyss.

The Art Nouveau riverboat glided to the pier like Charon's ferry in a movement reflected in the still water. The cabin had prettily patinated wood panelling. The light fixtures were brass, as was the helm. Beauty like this is growing rare everywhere.

Crickets were chirping in a clump of Turkish rocket. I had read that crickets could detect if someone had cancer from the smell of their breath before there was any other indication that they were ill. Such powers no longer hold any joy for me, whereas their chirping does.

On the riverbank, an elderly woman was breaking bread crumbs for the ducks with trembling fingers. Perhaps the ducks knew when to expect her. If she were to drop dead there and then, it would be a beautiful way to go. She had probably survived both Nazi and Red Army invasions, the latter twice.

The German soldiers hunted pigeons for food, to the consternation of the native Baltic population. In Lapland, I met a man who said that he had shot a crow with a sporting rifle as a child. He had plucked the bird and sold it to a German soldier as a grouse. Afterwards, the soldier pointed to the top of a pine tree, saying "Caw caw, nicht gut!".

Seeing old women in the streets of Berlin, I would muse about the horrors they had witnessed. My neighbour Marie had told me about them. What a stroke of luck it was to have been born after the end of the last wars and to die before our little globe becomes uninhabitable.

Seen from space, our planet, with its oceans, is breathtakingly beautiful, or so I am told. You can see the pyramids, but not the horrors perpetrated by humankind.

I walked on along the river. A carrion crow was feasting on a dead pigeon at the foot of a bronze statue of Pushkin. The crow's beak was red with blood. The famous author gazed into the distance proudly, perhaps hankering after the noble maidens he had chased.

In Odessa, Pushkin turns his back on his native country, dreamily facing the sea. As I stood before this statue, which was spattered with gull droppings, I felt like asking: "Brother Alexander, do you ever get bored up there?"

Pushkin's sea poems became symbols of unattainable freedom. Instead of venerating the power of the Tsars, he defended 'the small man' and called for mercy to the fallen. On the orders of Czar Nicholas I, Pushkin was interred in a monastery in the Pskov region rather than in St Petersburg, in an effort to avoid creating a pilgrimage site. The Czar thought people would never travel so far. He was wrong.

If Putin succeeded in his next attempt to murder Alexei Navalny, he would face the same problem, only much more vexatious.

On the edge of the footpath, another crow was pecking at a ping pong ball, which kept slipping to the side. Perhaps the crow thought it was a bird's egg with a particularly hard shell. In Berlin, I had seen a crow carry a walnut to a street junction where cars were waiting at a red light. When the light turned red again, the crow returned to eat the nut, which had been hulled by car tyres. In late autumn, crows migrate to Berlin, fleeing the cold winters in Eastern Europe. In the future, global warming will spare them the effort.

Behind a fountain, a small child learning to walk managed to stay upright for several tottering steps until reaching its mother's lap. The child beamed with pride at this feat. As I grew older, such sights increasingly brought me joy and a sense of continuity.

In one of Dostoevsky's works, the author discusses the problem of ageing people: how to preserve the freshness and sensitivity of one's emotions and recapture the alertness of a child. Many poets had a child's capacity for wonder.

When I quit my numbing day job, I became more aware of the nuances in memories, observations and emotions. I regained the alertness of a child. The world had not changed, but it seemed fresh. My future years stretched ahead, a landscape of unlimited opportunity. Life already seemed too short to find my place in it.

Although there were plenty of years in the calendar, my own years were now suddenly numbered and my alertness had begun to crack. I envied children their perception of time, which does not include an understanding of life's brevity. Apparently some people, when nearing the brink, regained their childhood faith. Why not, if it brought them comfort?

Even if I had been healthy, I still would have been growing older, and thus closer to death, by the minute. I also faced losing my beloved memories of a long, blessed life, which felt sad. The interval between childhood and old age had passed in the blink of an eye.

The boat, which had filled with tourists, floated downstream towards the sun. I bought a chocolate ice cream from a kiosk and sat down on a bench on the pier. A wagtail on the railing wagged its tail. Then it took wing and flew off towards the boat.

Church bells chimed in the distance. I had been taught that I should not ask for whom the bell tolls. Back in Berlin, around the corner from my flat, stood the Eliaskirche, which was no longer a functioning church, but it still tolled its bells out of habit. The chimes sounded bright, because they no longer called the congregation to worship.

I hovered between wakefulness and sleep, only roused when a tourist asked me in English about the riverboat schedules. I directed him to the other end of the pier, where there was a metal basket containing brochures.

I headed back for Vērmanes Park. Parks like this were havens of peace in the city centre, which was overrun with cars. I had not seen so many expensive cars in any other European metropolis. Driving them must have made life seem worth living after the Moskvitches, Pobedas and Trabants of old.

Groups of chess players had appeared near the stage, the sight I had been impatiently waiting for. The players, all male, straddled the benches or sat sideways with the board between them. Around them were rings of spectators, their faces revealing what they thought of the moves made and the positions on the board. Tobacco smoke filled the air.

These were men of my own grey generation. Everything about them spelled proletariat. There were no fashion magazine types. Their caps and sweatshirts spoke English.

I circled around among the players, watching the games unfold and trying to deduce from their appearance and style of play what sort of people they were. The predominant language seemed to be Russian, but mostly the players were silent. Almost everyone was playing blitz; only a handful of games were being played slowly, without a chess clock. Virtually every chess set looked different, unlike at most tournaments. Wooden pieces were giving way to plastic ones, and mechanical clocks to digital ones. The game itself had remained unchanged for centuries.

I sat down next to one of the boards. When the game was over, I said in Russian that I was a Finnish tourist and asked for a game. *Pozhaluysta!*

One of the men standing behind me muttered something about Finland being part of the western bloc that was harassing Russia with sanctions and trying to bring his country to its knees. He had a few teeth missing and his skin showed that he was no stranger to vodka. Perhaps he felt like a stranger in Riga.

I swore that I was innocent of the sanctions, and pointed out that Latvia was part of the same bloc – and a member of NATO to boot. My critic thought Latvia should leave both. As far as he was concerned, NATO membership was nothing but a joke.

My opponent had a pipe between his teeth. He only chuckled at the grumbler's complaints. He introduced himself as Arnis and set up the initial position.

– There we are, a three-minute game, Arnis said and blew a smoke ring.

– Would you mind five minutes? I asked.

– I'll fall asleep if we play so long.

– Okay, three minutes.

He put his pipe on the bench and opened with his king's pawn. I replied with the Sicilian Defence, and the game followed the usual course for a few moves, but then diverged into a side line leading to a position I was not familiar with.

An unusually large crowd had assembled around us; perhaps they were interested to see how well a tourist could play. I had not played in front of so many spectators since the tournament on the

Seven Seas a good half century earlier. Instead of schoolchildren, the ring around me now consisted of elderly pensioners. The *Seven Seas* had been scrapped, and some of the boys on that voyage had no doubt departed for heavenly pastures by now.

A collective sigh went up around me, signalling a bad move before I realized that I had made one. That single mistake was enough to lose the game. I set up the pieces again, stood up and bowed.

– Would you like a rematch? Arnis asked.

– A fair offer.

I opened with the Queen's Gambit. The position remained balanced, but in a complicated middlegame Arnis ran short of time, made some hasty moves and lost the game.

He proposed a third, decisive game. After some ups and downs, we reached an endgame position in which neither of us had enough pieces left to deliver mate, so the game was drawn. I thanked him for the games, and we shook hands.

– Does anyone here know Igors Rausis? I asked.

– The grandmaster who cheated, Arnis said. Gustav might know where to find him.

– Who is Gustav?

– One of us, but not here today. Maybe tomorrow.

– How does Gustav know Rausis?

– They shared a hospital ward.

Arnis lit his pipe and told me that Vērmanes was known as a chess venue all the way to America. Chess has been played in the park for a century, sometimes for money, even though the practice had been banned during the Soviet period. Many of Riga's best players had started out there, including Mikhail Tal, also known as Misha, the best of the lot.

When Misha was already world champion, he would sometimes come and watch amateurs play and analyse their games by way of instruction. Arnis said he had Misha's autograph, which he had framed and hung on the wall to accompany a gilt relief depicting the Kremlin. Misha had a long scar on his forehead at the time. In a bar in Havana, just before the Chess Olympiad began there, Misha, somewhat the worse for drink, flirted with a local woman in the bar. Her boyfriend hit him over the head with a bottle. Misha played the first rounds of the tournament with his head heavily bandaged.

According to Arnis, his friend Gabriels had kicked the bucket the spring before. Though not a great player, he had been an outstanding human being. He had worn the same leather cap adorned with a Lenin pin for half a century. On what had turned out to be his last appearance in the park, he had left his cap on a bench. Arnis had rescued it and was keeping it for the day when Riga sets up a chess museum.

Nowadays young people played chess on the web, so you did not see them in the park. Arnis thought online games and computer chess were the devil's invention. The top players had turned into computers. He was ready to confront a chess-playing computer, but only with a sturdy hammer in hand.

– What do you do for a living? I asked.

– Can't remember. It's so long ago.

– Arnis was a spy for the KGB, the man standing next to him said with a chuckle.

Arnis boasted that Riga's chess club used to be as strong as those of Moscow and Leningrad. The mighty Soviet Union had produced a string of world champions, although the greatest world champion of all, Bobby Fischer, was a Yank. Before Magnus Carlsen, no one had ever heard of Norway as a chess country; it was only known as a producer of petroleum and salmon. Carlsen beat Bill Gates in nine moves, which only goes to show how good Gates was.

– Do you have political arguments? I asked.

– Those are for the big shots. It's what they're paid for, Arnis replied.

– There is this guy who goes on about NATO and imperialist crooks.

– Sasha only watches Russian TV. Life hasn't been kind to him, but he's a good fellow.

People come to the park to play chess, meet friends, chat and have a picnic. Even a bit of rain will not stop the chess. Arnis quoted the motto of FIDE, the World Chess Federation: *Gens Una Sumus*, we're all one family.

– A family without a mother, I said.

– The motto may not apply everywhere, but it does here, Arnis replied.

The next day, the same men were playing on the same benches. Arnis said there was no sign of Gustav, and he did not have his number. Gustav would probably turn up one of these days unless he was ill or had gone on a bender. He was a passionate chess player, and the park was his favourite place.

I had read that Rausis had changed his name after he was caught. I did not know his new name, and even if I had, it hardly would have improved my chances of finding him. I would recognize him if I ran into him in the street, but the probability of that was as good as nil. If I could not find Gustav, the road seemed closed.

I wondered whether meeting Rausis would make any sense. He would not be able to save me or even help me, nor I him. Was my manic playing senseless, and was the whole trip to Riga nothing but a foolish whim and a deluded attempt to escape my fate?

It was one of those warm, sunny days that make you long for the seaside. Seeing the sea would not make my worries or disappointments go away, but I could hope for some relief. I also wanted to have lunch at the Majorenhoff pavilion, the seaside restaurant depicted on the postcard sent by my grandfather from Jurmala.

From the corner of the park, the railway station tower loomed in the distance. I walked towards it along the shady side of the street. The traffic lights next to the station had a counter showing the number of seconds left before the lights changed. Pedestrians had 13 seconds to cross the street. Every second after that would mean one second less for motorists. A car horn tooted at an old lady with a limp for whom 13 seconds was not enough.

Philosophers have tried to establish what time is. Whoever had programmed the traffic lights knew the answer, and apportioned time according to their car-friendly preferences. In informal games outside of official tournaments, the players themselves decide how much time to set on the chess clock, and it is up to them to ensure that it is enough for them to complete the game.

Perhaps there are as many different kinds of time as there are people who spend it. Life is the time control set for each individual. Its length is not determined by a zero-sum game, and only becomes known when the time is up. As for the identity of the programmer, opinions vary.

Dimly-lit, grubby tunnels led to the station. They were a gift to pedestrians from Soviet-era traffic planners, offering a safe and unobstructed route to the destination. Helsinki's central railway station had copied this concept.

I bought a return ticket to Jurmala's Major station. The booking clerk wrote down on the ticket the train's time of departure and the number of the platform, as well as the name of the station preceding Major, and showed me the way to the platform unasked. This could never have happened in the Soviet Union.

The train shook, jolted and squeaked. A mere handful of passengers sat on the blue and yellow benches. On the wall was an emergency brake handle and the words *avārijas bremze*.

On a train trip from London to Edinburgh, I had to pass through the first-class carriage to reach the restaurant car. The route illustrated Britain's strict class society. The hunters on a fox hunt do not get fleas from foxes. The inhabitants of Manchester's slums do.

The Soviet film *The Train Goes East* is set in the heyday of the Stalinist era in the Soviet Union. In honour of Victory Day, a dinner complete with shots of vodka is served to a diverse group of passengers, who join in singing songs extolling life's beauty in a class-free society. Moscow might be asleep, but Stalin is awake and thinking of his people even at this late hour.

The movement of the train sets the passengers' thoughts in motion, accompanying them like stowaways. For filmmakers, trains have inspired many a drama. They had also provided the setting for a number of short stories of mine published in a literary magazine, marking the beginning of my career as a writer.

I sipped from my mini-bottle of Riga Balsam, a black herbal liqueur tasting like cough medicine, and cast my mind back to past Interrail trips on which, crisscrossing Europe, I had struck up friendships that lasted many years.

The station announcements were preceded by a double ping reminiscent of clinking cowbells. A message from a bygone time that would never return.

Tree trunks fluttered past in the backlight. The train stopped at Zolitūde station. On the left were rows upon rows of miserable tenement flats, presumably from the Soviet period. It was a wonder that the authorities had approved such a realistic name. Arnis had said that he lived in Zolitūde, and that there was nothing to see. I immediately thought I must see this place. I would stop off on the way back from Jurmala.

I noticed a scratched, rust-spattered tin box on the floor marked *Whitman's Sampler Chokolade*. Inside it were hand-rolled fags giving off an intoxicating scent. The paper was translucent, the filters white as snow.

A young woman sat down next to me. Her hair shone in all the colours of the rainbow. She had tied up her ponytail with a rubber ring of the kind used for sealing jam jars. On her blouse, she wore a peace sign and a badge sporting the text *veģetārisms*.

Something about her reminded me of myself as a young man. I was still vegetarian, but with the same exception as Hitler: liverwurst. Adolf is also said to have eaten squabs, while I ate my surplus cockerels.

It was hard to imagine that one day this young woman would turn into a cynical housewife cosseting a greying husband. Whatever was in store for her, I would not be there to see it. What was she thinking of when she looked at me? Just one more of those egotists leading us down a blind alley and leaving a rotten world behind. Little could she know that I was measuring her years in the same despairing mood. We were of a piece.

In downtown Helsinki, I had run into a once-radiant friend who now stared ahead with bleary eyes and reacted to everything with *uh-huh*, *right* and *whaddya know*. I also knew people who still sparkled, even though their faces resembled a clay field in a drought.

The train dived into a birch grove dotted with old cottages with ornate woodwork and stacks of firewood in the yard. The scene looked like an old Russian film set.

The brakes screeched. The train stopped at Dzintar station, the one preceding Major. As I got up, the young woman smiled goodbye. I felt absolved. Her kind are the world's hope.

As soon as I reached the platform, I could hear the murmur of the sea. I walked along Jomas Street, which was lined by hostels, cafés, ice cream stands and souvenir shops. Pop music thumped from every direction.

I turned off into a dirt road leading to the seaside. Among the pine trees near the shore, traditional wooden holiday homes were interspersed with opulent villas protected by high steel fences from which security cameras protruded. *Nouveau riche* Russians had erected these villas with money stolen from the people. I was told you could build any monstrosity you liked as long as you knew the right people to bribe.

A crow cawed from the top of a pine tree, where it had built its nest without bothering to get a permit. The closer I came to the sea, the more hunched and skewed the pine trees were. Presumably that was how they shielded themselves from the strong winds. The sea glinted between the trees.

In a small seaside town, I once photographed a church for a book on Finnish wood architecture. I noticed that the church tower leaned. An architect friend of mine said that wood is a flexible building material that bends but does not break. However, he suspected the master builder may have made the tower lean on purpose to adjust to the prevailing westerly winds.

The beach was deserted, apart from one lonely soul loitering in the distance. There were no bathing huts, parasols or other signs of beach life. I looked for the Majorenhoff pavilion, but it no longer existed. The area was dominated by the concrete hulk of the Baltic Beach Hotel.

During the Soviet occupation, plastic packages containing bibles in Latvian were found on the beaches of Jurmala. Latvian refugees in Sweden had consigned the word of God to the waves in the hope that it would reach their compatriots. Now shreds of plastic floated towards the beach, the indestructible material that is suffocating our seas.

I bought a fish burger and a genuine Coca-Cola at a food stand by the beach. I rocked my chair and gazed at the open sea, which exuded cosmic peace. I could barely make out where the sea ended and the sky began.

The sea shimmered in shades of death. If only the wind and waves would carry off the frontier between life and death; if only I could listen to the splashing waves with no care for tomorrow.

I have asked my son to scatter my ashes in the sea from the cliff

I used to dive from as a child. This is forbidden, but there are no security cameras in the area. I have told him that there is to be no weeping at my funeral.

A bluish spinnaker swelled, as the boat it belonged to sailed off towards the open sea. I imagined that it was gliding towards Arcadia, a land where people lack for nothing, but have nothing in excess. Life is peaceful, all is clear and bright.

The vision made me want to jump aboard, but the boat was not within shouting distance. Besides, the shore was so shallow that a keelboat could not get anywhere near it. My grandfather must have landed his boat somewhere else.

Did he foresee the approaching war, did he hear the waves whispering of death as he stood there gazing out to sea? It was the end of August, and the Germans had just been stirring up provocations on the Polish border. Perhaps he thought he should not let the moment be spoiled by the threat of war.

He had already witnessed warfare in the Finnish Civil War in 1918. At the end of that war, he had been ordered to guard a group of Red prisoners to be interrogated. On Helsinki's "Long Bridge", they had met a German officer who had suggested it would be simplest to shoot the prisoners by the side of the bridge. My grandfather had replied: *Die Gefangenen sind meine Brüder*, the prisoners are my brothers.

When the Winter War broke out in 1939, my father was doing his compulsory military service in Viipuri near the Soviet border. He spent the next five years on the front, where death was everywhere and he no longer feared his own death.

Again and again, he would tell the story of what was the worst moment of the war for him. He was ordered to cross the straits between an island in the Gulf of Finland and the mainland, with a horse in tow. The horse was already on the shore when its hind legs were mutilated by a grenade, compliments of the peace-loving Red Army. He had to dispatch the screaming animal with his Luger. Its look as it awaited the *coup de grâce* kept haunting his dreams.

I would often think about how my father had been shaped by the war. He had been spared from trauma, but surely no one ever returned unscathed from the front line. Whereas I passed my youth in cafés discussing Nietzsche and Fellini, he had spent his best years in trenches and dugouts, where the topics discussed had been ruder. By the time the war ended, his youth was over, and he was in a hurry to start his engineering studies. He had neither the time nor the energy to philosophize, nor did such pointless pastimes inspire him later.

The country lay in ruins, but life had a clear direction that kept existential angst at bay. Unlike today, people believed that life would get better, and it did. Air supremacy reverted to seagulls and terns.

I stuffed the last bit of fish burger in my mouth and poured some more Coke. The bottle was the same shape as at the time of the Olympic Games in Helsinki in 1952, when I had my first sip of the murky wonder beverage. Some things still did not change.

The vendor came over to clear my table and complained about the scarcity of tourists. I asked whether he happened to have any information about Igors Rausis. He replied that he was British and the name meant nothing to him. He had always wondered why Latvian male names invariably ended in the letter *s*.

I was his age when I was discharged from the Finnish Army in spring 1968. On my last day of military service, I led a march as an officer cadet. As my platoon approached barracks, I placed white anemones in the marchers' rifle barrels, celebrating my release from the torture of barracks life and the mad Parisian spring, where demonstrators were calling for poetry and imagination to rule the streets.

My bullet-dodging father would have disapproved of my stunt. When the Soviet Union invaded Prague in the autumn of that same year, we agreed politically for the first time in my life. What did Rausis think of the occupation of his native Crimea?

The madness was temporary, or at least it changed: in curio shops in Paris, I later saw plastic paving stones sold as souvenirs. The slogans on the banners had taken on a hollow ring. Perhaps there was sand from the beach under the streets of Riga, too, but I no longer believed in achieving realism by demanding the impossible. Only private circles have enough space for utopia and experiments.

There was no call for rowdy behaviour in East Berlin at the time. As our Intourist guide attested, the new constitution of the GDR, enacted in 1968, guaranteed young people a free and happy life.

I started walking along the beach to Dubult, the next stop after Major. I stopped for a moment, scooped up a fistful of sand, and let it run out as if from an hourglass. Although there were grains of all colours, the sand all seemed to be of one colour, something I had wondered about since I was a child. The world was full of riddles. The mystery of the universe, too, could remain unsolved for all I cared.

In the indifference of space, we are mere grains of sand. Earth was five billion souls lighter than today when I was born. Even though there are ever more of us, the world's entire population would fit onto Lake Inari in Lapland, and the ice that covers it in winter would barely sag. Perhaps this might generate a feeling of internationalist and ecumenical solidarity that would end war and famine in the world.

I was at the *Skábmagovat* indigenous people's film festival in Inari one January on the occasion of the European premiere of a romantic comedy in the Hawaiian language. Young people cavorting on a sandy beach and making love under the palms. The temperature in Inari was -40 °C and the northern lights flashed over the spectators shivering in the Snow Theatre. The only place the director of the film had seen ice before was in his drink. He was a stout man, and did not dare risk a walk on the ice of Lake Inari, as he was afraid it would give way.

Once a Midsummer cruise I had booked to the humpbacked island of Ukonkivi in Lake Inari was cancelled because the lake was still frozen. The climate has a lot of warming to do before Lapland turns into a land of sleet and slush in winter, as has already happened in the southern parts of Finland.

The lack of islands and coastal cliffs made the Jurmala seascape monotonous. The glittering sea and the seagulls' cries reminded me of the island paradise of my childhood, where I burnt my skin every summer. That was probably the origin of my lethal disease.

The waves will still splash and the leaves rustle when I am gone. The gulls will be unaware of my passing. This continuity is comforting.

In my mind's eye, I saw myself sitting on a rocky shore with a fishing rod in my hand. The water was still crystal clear in those days. Seashells sparkled like tiny stars from a depth of four metres. I often yearned to be the little boy I once was, for whom all the world's wonders were free of shadows.

The island of my childhood had remained the constant setting of my dreams in which the departed shared adventures with the living. There was no separation between the here-and-now and the hereafter, merely a single unity. I wish it could be so in waking life, too.

No other landscape has ever aroused such a feeling of affinity in me. In the horizon, I could make out the contours of a craggy islet in the shape of a reclining woman, an image of continuity and immutability, a mirage rising up into the air as if pulled up by God. Perhaps this vision reflected the last traces of my childhood faith.

I never explored that little island. I feared that if I came too close, it would lose its charm and the enchantment would be broken.

I took off my shoes, tied the laces together, rolled up my trousers to the knees, and walked along the waterfront. The water was cool. I felt no inclination to swim.

I looked for small flat stones suitable for skipping, but could not find any. In a story I had read, a manic chess player was compared to a madman counting the pebbles on a beach.

A path led up from the beach to Dubult station. The station building was a sculpturesque concrete structure in the shape of a wave. A fluttering banner advertised an art exhibition on the theme of peace. This was what people had striven for throughout history, though with scant results.

The train was coming, and I only had time for a quick glance at the artworks. When I left, I asked the invigilator whether she happened to know anything about chess grandmaster Igors Rausis. She said the name sounded familiar, but could not say why.

She said she knew the Latvian managing director of the International Chess Federation, and could give me Dana's e-mail address. I thanked her for her kind offer, but said I had already sent Dana an e-mail, which she had not answered.

Back on the train, I took another sip of my Riga Balsam. When the conductor had checked my ticket, I leaned back in the corner of the carriage and dozed off. I only woke up when I heard the announcement for Tornakalns, the stop before Riga. See Zolitūde and die, I thought. I had not seen it.

A woman was sitting on the bench opposite, holding a stack of paper on top of a leather shoulder bag. When she turned a new page, I realized that the text was in English. She scribbled some question marks in the margin and underlined a few words. I wondered what the text was about and whether the butterfly on her earring was hand-painted. She had two point-shaped scars on her throat, as if she had been bitten by a viper. Was it possible to survive such a bite?

When our eyes met, I sensed curiosity and a kindred spirit. I wanted to ask her whether what she was reading was a script of some sort, but her gaze so impressed me that I was struck dumb.

When the train arrived at the main railway station, I lingered in my seat. The woman packed the papers in her bag, got up and stretched, and seemed to be searching for something to say. The carriage emptied. She smiled, wished me a nice day, and disappeared into the crowd.

I regretted my lack of initiative. I should have drunk my Riga Balsam down to the last drop right at the start of the journey. The image of her lively expression and the shape of her body still remained etched on my retina. I looked around for her instinctively in the thronging station. I would never see her again. If this had been a scene in a film, it would not have ended there, but the train and its passengers were bleakly real.

In the street, it occurred to me that I could have asked her about Rausis, too. Whether or not she knew about him, the conversation would have flowed on naturally, I was sure, and who knows what it might have led to? There would be no replay – once again.

I took a tour of the Zeppelin halls, which contain everything you might need one day, and a lot of things you will never need besides. There are lots of people who want it to be always Christmas.

The chiffon dreams in the clothing department were dashingly flared with nylon string. The range of bra colours was amazing. The stiff contours of the bras did not arouse erotic vibrations, unlike the bralessness of the woman on the train a moment ago. That kind of thing can stir you in a way that nakedness cannot.

It had been a dizzying moment for me when at a country dance I had first felt a woman's breasts pressed up against my dark suit. It had never felt the same again.

A bowl of cabbage soup and a serving of rhubarb fool cost a total of three and a half euros. I sat down with them in a wooden compartment supported by columns entwined with plastic wreaths.

In East Berlin, I had photographed the window display of a small shop consisting of a composition of red and white cabbages and a poster taped to the window extolling Karl Marx. Red cabbage cost 50 *pfennig* per kilo and white cabbage 40. At the Central Bank's department for trade with Eastern Europe, people always spoke about the "cabbage countries".

My rhubarb shoots originally came from the garden of the Romanovs. A friend of mine had inherited a clump of rhubarb crowns from his grandfather, who had worked as a gardener for the Tsar's family.

My once-thriving vegetable patch was now overgrown with burdock. The open gate of the chicken coop rattled in the wind. The droppings on the floor of the sheep barn evoked the memory of rams I had taught to butt. All this was sad, but life is not a supermarket.

I bought a couple of cabbage pies for supper and three bottles of Pumpurs beer. I knew nothing about Latvian beer, but the name sounded amusing, and I recalled that a poet by that name had written the Latvian national epic.

Thunder rolled, and the dark clouds boded rain. I hoped the TV in my hotel room would show some decent film in the evening that I could watch as I ate my pies and washed them down with Pumpurs. Maybe the beer would taste of Latvia's ancient history.

The skeletons in the *Dance of Death* fresco in Berlin's Marienkirche hovered in the shape of chess pieces. Skulls and bones gleamed in rainbow-coloured ripples of light filtered through the stained-glass windows. The organ rumbled thunderously.

When I opened my eyes, rain was dribbling down the window pane. The patter of rain is a comfortable sound, but not just now. There would be no games in the park, and it looked as though another day would go to the dogs. When I tended my garden, rain was a gift from heaven, as long as it did not go on for days on end. Zeus could not please everybody.

I lingered at the breakfast table. On the other side of the window, people maundered along the grey streets like sleep-walkers. At school, I once wrote an essay on work as the source of deepest happiness, echoing the words of my religion teacher. Nowadays I considered the elevation of work into an intrinsic value to be an aberration.

In my primary school days, a man was someone who did hard manual labour. People did not ask why they did the work they did. Work did not consist of the incompetent leading the unwilling to do the unnecessary. Work is lighter now, but working life is harder.

Women in sweatsuits sat at the neighbouring table, participants in some sports event perhaps. One of them was already consuming her second pot of raspberry yoghurt.

In the 1978 world championship match, Viktor Korchnoi, a defector from the Soviet Union, faced Anatoly Karpov, the defending champion. Korchnoi's team accused Karpov's aides of cheating by sending Karpov blueberry yoghurt, which they asserted was a coded message telling him to make a certain move. Before that, Karpov had already accused Korchnoi of trying to blind him with his mirrored sunglasses.

I turned on the TV in my room. A German channel was showing a documentary on the extinction of species and the loss of biodiversity. Overconsumption of natural resources and global warming had reduced Tellus to a critical state from which there was no return.

I read the day's newspaper on my iPad. A report on the municipal elections listed the crimes of which electoral candidates in the Helsinki region had been accused. The lead article called for intervention in the aircraft piracy practised by the Belorussian regime. The number of breast implants being removed already equalled the number of new ones. The sports page mentioned that one of the players on the national team had a thigh injury, but that his situation was improving daily. I stopped reading after this bit of news, since it promised a better tomorrow.

The rain had ceased and the clouds were beginning to disperse. The sun peeked out from a gap in the clouds. I went out and headed for Vērmanes Park. Cars were spraying the legs of any pedestrians who were not careful to stay close to the walls.

There were no chess players to be seen. I walked around the park, examining statues honouring Latvian dignitaries. The inscriptions were in Latvian, so the exploits they had been memorialized for remained a mystery. Not that there was any joy in it for them anymore, six feet under.

On the banks of the canal, I photographed a composition of three dancers holding hands. The anonymous dancers gave expression to a joy that can never be buried underground.

I walked on to the old town. Everyday life had abandoned the area, which looked like a pretty stage set. The central square was adorned with billboards and the plastic chairs of a pizzeria. A bright yellow Ferrari was parked in the courtyard of the Convent of the Holy Spirit.

Back at the hotel, I had been reading my grandfather's notes on Riga's old town. I realised how much had been lost. It was even more painful to read his descriptions of Jurmala. I would have to give up the idea of walking in his footsteps.

I had witnessed a similarly deplorable development in the old town of Warsaw, which I had first visited half a century ago. It had been throbbing with life then. One could find ordinary grocery stores, crafts workshops and little boys kicking a football there.

On that visit, I had met a Polish colleague for whom the traffic jams downtown symbolized progress. On his hardwood bookshelf, the Holy Bible stood next to a plastic miniature Volvo, a gift from a Swedish construction entrepreneur. He had hoped to buy a real Volvo in the near future. I gather that that particular dream had eventually come true.

I bought a chocolate ice cream and sat down on a park bench to enjoy it. A young man sat on the bench opposite, hits by The Animals blaring from his phone. His eyelids drooped. I turned my face to the sun and closed my own eyes.

When I tuned into the radio on my first morning in the United States in 1964, it was playing that band's brand-new recording of *The House of the Rising Sun*. For me, this grim story of a man destroyed by gambling represented a bright dawn at the threshold of adulthood. Ever since, hearing the song has carried me back to that moment, recreating the small town of Anoka in my mind's eye. Now that I no longer have a future, the past seems to be taking over.

I binned the ice cream stick and set off along the Daugava Promenade towards Vērmanes. In Venice, I had walked the Promenade of the Incurables. The name proclaimed the diagnosis, and must have gone back to the days of the Black Death.

Shafts of sunlight played on the surface of the water and were reflected back from the windows of the houses bordering the street. A group of smartly-dressed men entered Europe House. The warm day had not persuaded them to loosen their ties. Well, they were getting what they had bargained for.

Chess players had gathered on the park benches, and among one of the rings of spectators stood the man I had been hoping to find, the bear-like Gustav. He had been told I would be looking for him. He wore a Mercedes leather jacket that had once been white, with a pin showing a Trabant drawn with speed stripes and the word *Autorallye* stuck to it. His trouser legs flapped in the wind, adding to the impression of speed. He wore glasses repaired with duct tape and a butterfly-shaped bow fastened to the tip of his apostle's beard.

He was a head and a half taller than me and, to judge by his hands, had done honest work in his time. As we shook hands, I looked up at him and asked whether we had eaten the same soup as kids. He suspected he had been given a bigger spoon. I said that as it happened, I had not needed the room to grow into my first suit, but I was tall enough to see the stars in the sky.

I introduced myself as Matti. Gustav said the name was familiar from a play by Brecht that he had seen in his youth at Riga's Russian Theatre. He particularly remembered Herr Puntila, who climbed on the table when in his cups to praise Finland's nature. At an international youth festival in Rostock, members of a Finnish music group had taught Gustav to dance the *letkajenkka*.

– Finland's gift to the world in the art of dance, I said. What sort of man is Igors Rausis?

Gustav told me he had got to know Igors in hospital. Rausis had brain cancer, which he treated as a mere trifling ailment. He was friendly, and gave words of comfort to his fellow sufferers. He praised his treatment and the hospital meals. To hear him, the hospital sounded like a five-star hotel.

Gustav did not know where Igors lived, but had heard that he worked as a night guard for a security firm. He wrote the name of the company on the back of a receipt. I thanked him and put the receipt in my wallet. At least Rausis was still alive.

– Why do you want to find Igors? Gustav asked.

– I want to write a newspaper article about his career.

– You'll have the makings of more than one article.

– And what was it that led you to share a hospital ward with him?

– Liver cancer. It's getting worse and the pills are growing scarce.

– I'm sorry to hear it.

Gustav said that having read enough about the dangers of drinking, he had decided to quit – reading. Hardly anything had been written about the benefits. For him, cancer was a reasonable price to pay for the joys of vodka, and he had no regrets. He was still accepted as a blood donor, but he had no wish to become a model citizen.

– *Khorosho*, I said.

Gustav said he had smuggled a vodka bottle into the hospital. The doctor, a drinker himself, only chuckled when he saw it. Gustav offered Igors a sip, which was politely refused. Igors had Tolstoy's *Anna Karenina* on his bedside table; Gustav had a porn magazine.

I said that Russians who refused a drink should be preserved and put in a waxworks museum. I had heard of priests sprinkling holy water over the city of Tver from a helicopter. The ceremony was supposed to protect the citizens from the ills of liquor. The story did not tell whether the plan had worked.

– Ha ha, drink what you will, you'll die anyhow, Gustav said. Same thing if you abstain.

One of the men asked him for a game. Gustav reminded me of a Finnish friend who had been in a similar situation, with no concern for the consequences of drinking. Drunk and sober, he was two different people who barely knew one another. Life without drinking was not worth living as far as he was concerned. He died, but not of boredom.

I wondered what diseases and death sentences lay behind this brotherhood's games. One of them had said he was living on borrowed time, without specifying what he meant. Probably not many among them had been spared prostate problems. No doubt a few seats would be vacant by next summer. Prattling about golden years and the gift of life's transience seemed like burying one's head in the sand.

Playing chess did not impose total silence, but it released the players from the obligation to talk. If chess had not been invented, they might have played cards, but that probably would not have given rise to so much solidarity. Though perhaps I was merely idealizing the royal game.

Light and shadow played on the rough surface of the stone tables. I sat down next to one table, looked up the phone number of the company Gustav had mentioned, keyed in the number and asked for Rausis. The man who answered was sorry, but he could not reveal any information about employees. What next? Gustav could give me the name of the hospital, but there the rules on data protection would be even more stringent. A dead end, I thought.

Gustav challenged me to a game. He said he had grown slower with age, and the five-minute time control suited him. As he was setting up the pieces, he told me he had shown his juniors what's what when he won the Ziemelski district championship in beautiful Alekhine style. He had endured a whole week without imbibing a drop, but had made up for this once the tournament was over.

– What did you get for a prize? I asked.

– An apple and a bottle of Moskovskaya vodka.

– An apple?

– That was to encourage a healthy lifestyle.

– Do you still have the bottle on top of your sideboard?

– Yup, filled with water.

He had the same kind of chess clock as the one I had bought in Leningrad half a century earlier. I could have bought two electronic clocks for the price of having the old one repaired, but I could not bear the thought of giving it up. It crystallized the enchantment of a thousand games. The enchantment will be broken the moment I die.

The sun was blinding me. I pulled down the brim of my hat to shield my eyes.

– *Gotovyi li vy*, are you ready?

– *Da*, I replied.

He played more aggressively than I did, but I realized quickly that we were equally matched. I saw in his eyes that the realization was mutual. When moving, he banged the piece on the board so hard that the other pieces shuddered. He kept glancing at the clock, and when his time began to run out, his hand hovered above the piece he intended to move next. This was against the rules, but I preferred not to remind him.

Gustav's sighs gave away whenever he thought he was in trouble during a game. He would also drum his temples with his fingers. Whenever he made a bad move, he would sniff in disgust, helping me to discover the mistake. It was always harder to play against a poker face.

After four games, each of us had won two with the white pieces. Two men commented on the positions in Latvian, occasionally giving Gustav advice. In the fifth game, which we had agreed would be the decider, Gustav opened with the Queen's Gambit, which is what I usually played with white. I knew what to do, and played my first moves at lightning speed. The game progressed as usual until I made a beginner's mistake: I allowed Gustav to give check with a knight, depriving me of the right to castle. Gustav had enough time on his clock to win the game, and I resigned.

I thanked him for the games and made room for the next player. The games with Gustav had not been a battle of egos. I had tried to win, but the result did not matter. This made playing against him innocuous. I liked his gallows humour.

When I played my friend Daniel, my body remained tense after every two-hour blitz session, and I was unable to concentrate on anything significant. I could understand chess masters who would go on a bender at the end of a tournament.

With Daniel, the rage to win was mutual, but we swallowed our losses stoically and appreciated each other's strong moves and ingenious variations. There was more pleasure in losing a good game than in winning a poor one.

I sat down on a bench a little way off and dialled the same number, introducing myself by a different name this time. The phone was answered by another service representative. I said I was a Finnish IT entrepreneur and had already set up offices in five different EU countries. I was now planning to do the same in Riga. I needed to consult them on data protection, and would later also require security guard services. We set up a meeting for the following day.

At the end, I mentioned that I had heard that the former chess grandmaster Igors Rausis was working for the company. I said I had played him at a tournament in Finland in the 1990s and hoped to meet him. The representative told me the location of the shack from which Rausis worked night shifts as a security guard.

The map application on my phone showed that the building site was located about five kilometres away from my hotel. It gave me a good excuse to head in another direction than downtown Riga.

I turned on the TV in my room. CNN was running a report on the desperate situation in Yemen. I switched to a channel where the Pope exhorted us to show love and mercy. I switched again, and found myself watching a local football match while waiting for the evening. The match meant nothing to me, and this was not a fruitful kind of idleness. I felt guilty about wasting my dwindling allocation of time like this.

I spotted a dead fly on the window sill. Yesterday, it had buzzed against the glass, although that could have been another individual. When flies die, they fall on their back with their legs up in the air. I swept the fly into the bin, packed my umbrella and glasses in my shoulder bag, and went out.

My destination was close to a bus route, but I preferred to walk. I assumed that Rausis would be spending the time between doing his rounds in the shack. How would he react to an unknown person knocking on the door? Would he have a gas spray handy?

Screams of swifts streaked across the sky, wings gleaming in the evening sun. They darted in and out among the trees, soaring up from time to time, mere dots against the blue sky. Swifts can actually fly in their sleep. Do they die in mid-flight, too?

Back in Kirkkonummi, I had built a couple dozen boxes for swifts to nest in, hanging them five metres up birch trees. The birds arrived in mid-May and left at the beginning of August. Finland was just a wide-open maternity ward for them.

Left untended, nest boxes will rot, and their sickle-winged denizens will have to find new lodgings. I myself had also sought new lodgings, which was small consolation to the swifts. I had no idea why the swift's silhouette accompanied some death notices and why metal sparrows were placed on some headstones.

The house numbers told me I was approaching my destination. The plaster on the nearest apartment house had flaked like sunburn. A hammer had already been taken to the façade, but I could still see the red, spray-painted heart on it. A forgotten shirt swung in the wind on a clothes line.

I went round to the back of the house. Rusty pipes climbed up the wall like veins. I made out the contours of a tiled stove inside. The smell of coal fumes was gone, the souvenirs on the mantelpiece had been stored away, and the occupants' dreams had moved house. The scene reminded me of some previous experience, but I could not tell what it was. Perhaps I had seen it in a dream.

This had been a home where people watched the sun rise and set, admired frost flowers on the window panes, sniffed the smell of fried fish, heard children crying or laughing next door, and listened to the patter of rain and the chatter of sparrows.

What sort of impressions did this sight awaken in the former occupants, if indeed they were still alive? Did they look upon it with tears in their eyes, or did they perhaps give it a wide berth? Rausis himself would probably never want to see even a photograph of the pavilion where he had played his last tournament.

I fumbled in my mind for a way to approach him. I was hoping for a fit of clear-headedness, but it did not arrive. The people who had met him had described him as amiable, but I could imagine that his suspicions would be aroused by someone popping up out of the blue. Perhaps he would categorically refuse to discuss what had transpired in Strasbourg. He must also surely realize that no one would have taken an interest in his chess career and life if he had not cheated.

Perhaps he would suspect that I was going to write yet another sensationalist story about the disgraced master fallen upon hard times. If he rebuffed me, I could still spend a few days playing chess in the park, although that would seem like a poor substitute. Perhaps I would change my flight for an earlier date.

Except for its parks, Riga did not inspire me as a city, although skimming through a book of 1930s photographs, I had understood why my grandfather had called it the pearl of the Baltic. Jurmala, too, had looked divine in those days. The past was beautiful and gentle, in this case even without the gilding of memory, but it could not be attained by walking backwards.

Perhaps I had only chanced upon uninteresting places. No doubt there were lively taverns, underground events and snug corners in secret alleyways, but Gustav & Co would hardly be the best guides to them.

Perhaps the filter through which I saw the city was clouded by my illness. If I had arrived one year earlier, my reaction might have been completely different. I would not have wasted my time sitting in front of the TV in my hotel room, which was something I had mocked others for doing.

Be that as it may, these abandoned, derelict buildings were more interesting than the polished modern downtown area. Perhaps I saw myself as their companion in misfortune. Their days were also numbered.

I noticed a birch sapling sprouting from a ruined balcony. Its leaves would soon take on their deepest green colour, which would last for a short while. Perhaps the house would be bull-dozed before the birch could celebrate in autumn colours.

A birch tree grew in the courtyard of the Church of the Holy Trinity in Helsinki. I could see it from my office window. It had no emotions, and the only purpose of its existence was to remain standing. A thrush had built its nest in the fork of the trunk. A magpie often settled on one of the branches. It seemed to be laughing at me.

When I was trying to make up my mind to leave my job in the bank, my friend Ilpo said that if you don't do what you're think-ing of doing in time, you'll soon find yourself not thinking at all. This sentence was echoing in my head at a book fair when a former colleague grabbed me by the sleeve. He was in a wheelchair. He was disfigured by disease, and I was embarrassed not to have recognized him at once. He had become used to having to remind acquaintances who he was.

We went to the cafeteria. He had planned to build a wooden rowboat modelled on one his father made after taking retirement. His idea was to row the boat along the coast of the Gulf of Finland to his ancestral home on an island off Kotka. He never made that trip, and all that was left for him was pain-filled old age.

He was one of those dutiful souls who were needed to get the bank's essential work done and to keep the economy turning. He was not familiar with either Ingmar Bergman or Thomas Mann. He had no use for such knowledge. He considered himself useful and his existence meaningful. As for me, I was an ungrateful whinger and a daydreamer floating around in a fantasy world.

He knew about my chess playing, which he thought was a waste of intellectual capacity. He thought I could have found better uses for my brains. Occasionally I thought the same.

Disease had also marred the good looks of the chess wizard Mikhail Tal. At the tail end of his life, he met a close chess colleague in a park. The latter greeted Misha and asked him how he was. In reply, the former world champion embraced his comrade, grateful for having been recognized. The statue I saw in Riga, on the other hand, depicts Tal in the flower of youth.

Perhaps I would wind up like Tal. I consoled myself with the thought that as a deserter from monetary policy I was no longer unwell because I did things I did not want to do, or living from one weekend and holiday to the next. In this respect at least, I had no regrets.

Changing profession and hometown had opened up my life and extended my time. There was no power that could stop time entirely, though. My diagnosis reduced the time left to me even further.

The birch tree on my balcony in Berlin had grown taller and stronger. I had moved it to a bigger pot, and it had made use of the extra soil to grow. It had become a holy tree for me. Every time its leaves began to sprout in the spring, I wondered how many times I would experience the thrill of this moment again. This question, too, had taken on a whole new meaning.

Perhaps on the brink of death I would use the twigs of my home birch to make a sauna whisk – that is, if the Grim Reaper deigned to arrive in summertime. Whisking prepares you for the transition from existence to the void.

The signs of life were increasingly few and far between. A cloud of acrid smoke rose from a pile of twigs pierced by the sun's diagonal rays. I realized that I was entering a waste land dotted with dandelions. The address indicated by the security guard was behind my back. I had cancelled my appointment with the security firm, telling them I would postpone setting up office to the autumn.

In my student days, I had realized early on that I did not have what it takes to be a businessman, for both ideological and neurological reasons. Running a chicken coop did not involve either.

I reversed my steps and noticed a path leading to a gated housing estate under construction. The houses were obscured by leafy trees. The yards were full of scaffolding, machinery, piles of planks and miscellaneous junk. A shack stood at the edge of the area, but behind a locked gate. So this was where Rausis spent his nights.

As I approached, I saw a human figure sitting in the shack. It was not Rausis.

I gesticulated towards him, but he did not look up. I threw a pine cone at the window. When the man appeared at the door, I called out in Russian to tell him why I was there. He opened the gate and said that Rausis was in hospital for tests, but maybe he would be back tomorrow.

Maybe tomorrow... I sincerely hoped that Rausis would not turn out to be another Godot. I shut the gate behind me and sat down on the rough trunk of a felled pine tree. I counted the annual rings on the stump. They grew thinner from year to year. The tree was one year older than me at the time it was cut down. I calmed myself: a stump is just a stump. It was pointless to seek meaning in something that had none.

If I had had a Finnish belt knife on me, I would have cut out a sizeable chunk of bark from the pine trunk and whittled it into a sailing boat. In my mind's eye, I saw myself launching it in the canal that runs through Kronvalds Park, then watching it bob away, vanishing into the backlight. A brief moment of childhood happiness, a return to the perfection of being open to the world.

When still in primary school, I cut out a comic strip from a newspaper to make a sail for a bark boat, undaunted by the death notice on the reverse side. For the rudder, I used a penny coin with edges sharpened by leaving it on a tram track.

Nowadays, when reading death notices in the paper, I kept finding familiar names; oh really, her too, and that fifty-year-old who had such a healthy lifestyle, whatever killed them? Life is a game of Russian roulette.

If there happened to be no familiar names among the notices, I thought I had wasted my time reading and felt a pang of conscience for my inability to be happy about it. While grieving for the departed, I reminded myself that most of the people I knew were still clinging on to life.

The man from the construction site opened the gate and drove out in his Audi. The fence was evidently intended as permanent, which was the case in many suburban neighbourhoods in the metropolises of Eastern Europe. Open days were over. I had attached the metal logo of a GDR car on the door to my chicken coop. States were no longer fenced off in Europe, nor were correctional labour camps fashionable anymore. Nonetheless, followers of the prevailing ideologies were setting up barriers around their cliques everywhere.

In many countries, statues of Lenin had been hoisted away by cranes and stored out of sight. Experienced sculptors had been able to sculpt them blindfold. In Russia, Stalin was being honoured with new statues that were admired even by people whose family and relatives had been killed or sent to prison camps under Stalin's orders. Putin & Co played down Stalin's misdeeds while building up their image of a brilliant, irreproachable motherland. In Russian literature, statues walked of their own volition, but they ignored the ups and downs of politics.

I bit into an apple I had snapped up from the hotel's breakfast buffet and hidden in my bag. The idea had occurred to me when I was at the table, and I kept thinking about it until doing the deed. In his interview, Rausis had given a similar explanation for cheating in Strasbourg.

When German tourists used the hotel buffet spread to assemble their meals for the whole day, they went a step too far. One was always tempted to draw the line such as to place oneself on the side of the angels.

In the morning, I had seen a woman drop a slip of paper on the pavement. A man walking behind her picked it up, caught up with her and handed her the piece of paper with a smirk on his face. What if she had dropped a fifty-euro note? If you find one in the street, there is no one to give it back to, and taking it to the lost and found office benefits no one. You are spared a dilemma and can slip the note in your wallet with a good conscience.

According to the interview, Rausis felt guilty about what he had done in Strasbourg. That is what I would have said in his place, but I am not sure I would have agreed to give an interview. Conscience is an adaptable mutant, capable of digesting a wide variety of doctrines and precepts, which it can apply and interpret to its own advantage. Some people have a lump of ice in place of a conscience. They are not troubled by shame or remorse and sleep undisturbed by these ancient sentinels.

The light nocturnal breeze stirred up a whiff of damp earth. I broke off a dandelion stem and blew at the downy tuft. The wind carried the hairs in the direction of the shack. A window flashed as a man opened it to light a cigarette. Similar container shacks could be found on building sites, stacked up to provide shelter for workers. I once built a three-storey nest box for starlings, but only the top floor was good enough for them. People were not so picky.

Back home in Finland, I had dismantled a disused wooden shack on a building site, reassembled it in my backyard and used it as a chicken coop. I had gone to the outdoor market after business hours to collect leftover vegetables and roots. The owners of a granary had given me permission to sweep up surplus oats from the floor. The bank's canteen staff had saved up bread crusts that I packed in a sack and carried with me on my commute from the fog of the national economy to the transparency of chicken husbandry. Chickens were real.

I had been induced to build a chicken coop by reading a handbook on rearing poultry, found in the attic of a deserted house in Porkkala. The family who lived there had been obliged to leave when Finland had to lease the area, which was within firing range from Helsinki, to the Soviet Union in 1944. The Soviets left in 1956, but the family never returned; perhaps they had died by then.

The handbook emphasized that chickens are sociable creatures that like to hear their owner's friendly chatter. The book reflected the spirit of the era, a period of scarcity, a spirit we can no longer afford in our times of plenty.

In the morning I explored the world-renowned Art Nouveau buildings in the hotel neighbourhood. My eyes registered mythological figures, wreaths, female torsos and geometric reliefs on the façades. A fairytale peacock was about to take wing just above a balcony.

A muscular male figure was holding up a bay window on a street corner. His expression was anguished in the manner of Edvard Munch's painting *The Scream*. Was this because of the weight of the window or of life in general?

Did this opulent ornamentation express a longing for something lost? For lack of points of reference, the abundance began to gall after I had viewed a few blocks. Homely bears, owls, pine cones and water lilies were more in step with nature and my own mood.

I bought a ticket for ten journeys at a public transport booth. The ticket bore a photograph of the River Daugava, which runs through Riga. Instead of a cross, the spire of St Peter's Church on the riverbank sports a rooster, an ancient symbol of wakefulness and the bane of ghosts: Watch therefore, for ye know neither the day nor the hour.

My own rooster always reminded me of the pictures in my alphabet book. All it knew was a blissful country life unsullied by urban din and sin. A drawing in the book showed mother and child waving to father, who is tilling a field. For the father, the harder the work, the greater the peace of mind. This matched my experience from the time when I built my house and chicken coop.

I reached a tram stop and boarded the first tram. It was covered in advertisements for potato crisps. Some crisps lay on the floor.

Nikita Khrushchev, pal of Finland's president Urho Kekkonen and veteran of neck shots, went to school for two winters. His father paid the priest eighty pounds of potatoes for the privilege. One wonders whether it was Nikita's laziness or an empty potato bin that put an end to his schooling.

As a child in 1957, I sat on the sauna terrace with a pair of binoculars and watched Urho and Nikita on the deck of a ship sailing past our island. The two gentlemen once had a sauna session that lasted until 5 am. Khrushchev received a reprimand from the Central Committee: Stalin never would have bared his buttocks to a capitalist. Khrushchev replied that he would rather negotiate treaties stark naked with Kekkonen then fully dressed with Hitler.

In Potsdam's Sanssouci park, I once spotted a few potatoes on King Frederick's tomb, a belated token of gratitude from a passer-by to Old Fritz for having brought the potato to Prussia and thus saved the people from starvation.

At first, everyone on the tram sat alone, but at each stop, more people got on than off. People only took a seat next to someone else when there was no alternative. This appeared to be a general practice, at least in western countries.

I instinctively looked out for the woman who had sat opposite me on the train. This encounter had briefly reawakened a rage for life that still lingered and almost made me forget my despair when I drank my Pumpurs beer at the hotel.

I tried in vain to suppress my vexation at this missed opportunity. I remembered once debating in my mind whether I dared open the catch on my girlfriend's bra. Then as now, feelings of intimacy and insecurity had vied for prevalence. This had been my first experience of touching the rounded shape of bare shoulders and breasts.

When the buildings passing by became more humdrum, I got off. Cars whizzed past in an unending stream. After walking for a moment, I boarded an old-fashioned blue and white tram. I did not know where it was going, but since I was not going anywhere, I could hardly go astray.

The tram was powered from above, that much was indisputable. As we rattled over a bridge of the River Daugava, the shimmering water was reflected from the roof. A barge floating past under the bridge spat out smoke rings, as if its engine was smoking a pipe.

On the opposite shore, Riga's skyline loomed, punctuated by a handful of box-like hotels mocking the church towers. Helsinki, too, had let tower blocks fracture its skyline, banishing its commercial harbour, the source of my summer earnings, from the city centre. The landscape of my childhood now existed only in old photographs and films.

We had been tricked to believe in the inevitability of change, and the Green Party were at the forefront of this swindle. The political had disappeared from politics, depriving elections of all interest. However, it was still wrong to equate non-alignment with indifference.

Bulldozers were threatening my rural landscape in Kirkko-nummi. The mere threat of destruction would have poisoned what remained of my life if I had stayed. Again, I concurred with Chekhov: the most intolerable people are local luminaries.

The leafy district around Helmholtzplatz, dating from the period of Kaiser Wilhelm, represented stability. Sitting on a bench in the park, my mind filled with peace. Every house bordering the park was distinctive, just like human beings are.

The tram lurched on, skirting a wide meadow dotted with dandelions until it reached a group of run-down wooden houses. A few of them had well-tended gardens. Lilacs and bird cherry trees blossomed all around, forming a fairytale scene. What would it look like in the November sleet? As soon as this thought occurred to me, I wondered why. Here and now.

The names of the tram stops meant nothing to me. In Halle, I once rode the world's longest tram line from end to end. Seated in one of the cosy carriages, I photographed the name of a stop as it appeared on the display: *Frohe Zukunft*, Happy Future. In the GDR era, that particular district was best known for a prison crammed with young people and children.

I got off at the terminus to stretch my legs. I bought a doughnut and a cup of bitter coffee at a kiosk, then returned along the same route. I continued like this for hours on end without trying to produce a consistent story from my fragmentary impressions. Sometimes life itself felt like aimless drifting.

I had done the same in Prague, Budapest and Warsaw. The difference was that not a single house or neighbourhood in Riga brought back memories for me, and I would hardly have time to create new ones here. Only the screeching rails evoked a faint recollection. I wondered which remote corners of Helsinki I would be roaming if I knew my last days were at hand. I would see them through the eyes of a tourist, even though memories would be surging up at every turn.

Cities that were split by a river and had a tram network always awakened warm feelings in me. The cities of Eastern Europe had had the sense to keep their tramways. I was old enough to have enjoyed tram rides in Stockholm. The conductor reigned on her high stool like a queen, ordering the passengers to move forward. On a tram in bilingual Helsinki, I had learned my first Swedish sentence: *Framåt på gången*, forward in the aisle – not a bad maxim.

This particular tram was an angular eyesore, but it would take me to my destination just as surely. I observed the passengers and wondered about their moments of joy and sorrow. What did they still dream of? I could distinguish fragments of sentences in Russian: everyday chatter. The conversations in Latvian, however, remained background noise, which felt somehow liberating.

A man was feeling his cheek: could he be heading for the dentist's rack? A woman held a bunch of tulips in her lap: perhaps she was on her way to meeting a friend. She gazed wistfully at the sparkling river. Her handbag was inscribed, in gilt lettering, with the words Versace Jeans Couture. That kind of finery was alien to my generation.

She had painted her nail extensions and lips scarlet. My sister had learned in Sunday school that lipstick was made from cockroach blood. The Nazis had banned lipstick, but that was hardly the reason. The ban did not apply to Leni Riefenstahl, one of Hitler's favourites. She denied all knowledge of the Holocaust. Bobby Fischer, who admired Hitler, was convinced that the Holocaust never happened.

The men sitting in front of me were talking in Russian. I wondered which part of the Soviet Union they or their parents had been shipped in from. From their rough demeanour and Adidas outfits, I deduced that they did not belong to the country's original Russian population. Similarly, I believed that I could tell the *nouveaux riches* apart from old money.

The tram turned into a side street. No more piles of coal here, either, but from the open window came a whiff of brown coal, the odour of East Berlin. There I could still find the ambience of the Helsinki of my childhood: shop windows exuding a sense of innocence, coal heaps in the street, eastern cars. I slept more peacefully in those days than I ever did as an adult. The smell of a lumpy straw mattress also transported me decades back in time.

Gone, too, from Riga were the Soviet-era pyramids of tinned food, the soap packets decorated with carnations, and the fanned sets of socks that I had photographed in Tallinn. When I took shots of customers queueing up in front of shops, a *militsiya* patrolman tore the film out of my camera. The same thing happened in Leningrad when I was retracing Dostoevsky's footsteps in Sennaya Square. The *militsiya* told me that the old women selling their wares took my camera for an evil eye.

In Prague in 1988, I was thrown in jail for a day when I photographed a counter-demonstration to the May Day parade. A young woman was brought into the same cell. Judging by the peace symbol she was wearing and her hippy look, she had been picked up at the same event. We sat on a bench like birds on a wire. Although we had no common language, we managed to develop one as the day went by. I observed Jitka approvingly and tenderly like a father watches over his child. I assumed that the arrest would mean trouble for her; for me, it was just an amusing footnote to my album of memories. In Russia, a member of the intelligentsia who has not been arrested is not worth a kopeck.

I got my camera back, but the exposed film roll in it was gone. So I lost my shots from the top floor office in the electrical company Elektromont's building, where Kafka had worked as an official for an accident insurance institution, staring out of the window at Na Poříčí street below. I did not succeed in wangling my way past the peak-capped doorman a second time.

An electrical engineer was sitting in Kafka's office. He told me that Kafka was no longer completely banned, but that you could not find his books anywhere in Prague, ostensibly owing to a shortage of paper. Printing cost money; unprinted texts earned money. For a Czech author in those days, it was shameful to have your books sold in bookshops.

The engineer told me that the real reason was that the country's best-known Kafkalogist was in trouble with the authorities. He mentioned in passing that he himself was an amateur actor. He had recently played a supporting role in a production based on *The Trial*.

The man sitting next to me said something in Latvian. I told him in Russian that I did not speak his language. He asked me in Russian whether the tram would pass such and such a crossroads. I said I did not have the slightest idea where we were going. He stared at me in perplexity, no doubt wondering what institution the old geezer had run away from.

A note on that jail visit had been the only entry in my Stasi file. The cops in the socialist countries warned each other of threats to the system. I had been perceived as a threat, albeit on shaky grounds.

At my university, my name had wound up on a blacklist kept by the private business sector. This list (which officially did not exist) contained the names of students who were politically suspect. I heard about it from a fellow student whose father was the manager of a paper mill. This piece of news marked the high point of my student years.

My faith in real socialism had already flagged as a result of the occupation of Prague in 1968. The faith of one of my close friends remained unshaken until the collapse of the Soviet Union, which resulted in his own collapse. He had been convinced that communism, which was still in its building phase, would eventually lead to an affluent world in which the air was easier to breathe. The national economy would give way to a nationalized economy.

He was aware that the shops in socialist countries tended to run out of stocks from time to time. As housing was inexpensive, the population had plenty of purchasing power. Meanwhile in the West, the shop shelves sagged under the weight of goods because people could not afford to buy them. As far as he was concerned, this capitalist heaven had no future.

On a visit to Berlin, he bought some Bohemian crystal to bring back to his mother. He admitted that it was petty bourgeois kitsch, but then again you did not have to look at the world through a black and white lens. The most important thing was to keep your thinking crystal clear.

The shop windows in Riga were pasted full of garish advertisements, as they were in other civilized countries. No light of day reached the interiors. A former butcher's shop in Berlin offered laser tattoo removal, while a fishmonger's had been converted into a nail salon. We do not live on bread alone.

Next to a tram stop, I spotted an undertaker's window with white lace curtains and a coffin decorated with roses. The mere thought gave me claustrophobia.

The chess automaton built by Wolfgang von Kempelen had a dwarf-sized chess master inside who operated a complex mechanism to direct the moves executed by the mechanical doll sitting above him. The turban-headed automaton, dressed in Ottoman robes, attracted wonder and fear. It defeated chess masters and statesmen, including Napoleon Bonaparte and Benjamin Franklin.

The graves in Hietaniemi, Helsinki's principal cemetery, were still being dug and filled manually. One of the gravediggers used to keep a dish brush on his belt for cleaning skulls as he searched for earrings and gold teeth, which he would then exchange for liquor.

On a remote back road during a moped journey across Finland, I encountered an old man driving a Wartburg car and asked him for instructions to the nearest shop. He told me and said his Eisenach beauty was his fourth car of the same make. He had had his first sexual experience in the back seat of one. He would complete his journey in this specimen and then dig a hole that was big enough to fit both him and his car. When Resurrection Day is here, all graves will open far and near, he said with a twinkle in his eye.

Would Rausis want his favourite chess pieces to be buried with him? Would they reawaken memories of brilliant games played around the world, or would they invoke shame and repentance? Perhaps he would ask for the sea shells he had collected on the beaches of Sevastopol.

Once out of the city centre, we passed clusters of small houses, sports fields, car parks and empty, grass-covered lots. Once again I felt the combination of distance from my customary haunts and idle time in a foreign city condensing into some essence of the past. Such aimless wanderings had previously served to generate purpose; they now had a bitter aftertaste.

I got off the tram and asked a stranger the way to downtown Riga. She said it was an hour's walk and recommended a bus, as there was a bus stop just a stone's throw away. I replied that I had plenty of time, which was a half-truth. Time is endless, but a human being's time is limited.

The sun warmed the back of my shirt. I realized that I was following my shadow. When the sun hid behind a cloud, my dark companion disappeared, but I kept walking in the same direction.

A one-legged man sitting in front of an ATM machine was playing an operetta tune on his melodica. A dog lay curled up at his feet. In front of him was a Starbucks paper cup containing a few coins. The man cast imploring looks at passers-by. Perhaps he was a veteran of the Afghanistan war.

In Berlin, I often saw a man sitting in front of an ATM with his dog. Sometimes I would drop a coin in his cup. Late one night, he got up to stop me and asked why I never spoke to him.

In Leningrad, our tour guide informed us that there were no beggars in the Soviet Union. Nonetheless, we spotted a few during the tour. The guide said they had acted as informants for Hitler's fascists during the wars, and the State therefore had no obligation to look after them. A Russian artist friend of mine said he had learned in school that all Finns were fascists and that all capitalists were leeches.

I remember a man playing an old wartime tune on the harmonica in the backyard of the house I lived in as a child. My mother wrapped a few coins in a piece of paper and threw it down from the window. One of his trouser legs hung empty. He said he had stepped on a mine laid by Finland's united and mighty neighbour country. Living as a cripple was cumbersome, but it could still be a full life, and it was not shortened by the lack of a leg.

I turned off the street into a park. A young woman came up to me and gazed into my eyes, speaking nonstop. First I thought she wanted money, then I concluded she must be a preacher from some religious sect. Her words sounded tuneful, and her eyes glowed with warmth. When she finished her speech, she slapped me on the shoulder and went off, skipping like a little girl.

The language was probably Lithuanian. Perhaps she had been reciting a long poem or words of wisdom. Whatever it was, it felt good, and dispelled the last remnants of horror from my mind.

I recognized Igors Rausis from some way off. Having learned my lesson from the train trip to Jurmala, I took a sip of liquid courage from my hip flask. That is what I had done at country dances back in the old days.

I went up to the fence and threw a pine cone at the window of his shack. Rausis glanced up, limped to the gate, leaning on a walking stick, and keyed in the code to open the lock.

I explained in English who I was, where I was from and how I was fascinated by the world of master chess, knowing that he was well-versed in chess history and legend. I told him I was an amateur player with a particular interest in the cultural history of chess, but that I still had a long way to go to becoming a grandmaster.

Rausis chuckled and wished me welcome to Riga. His handshake was firm and warm, which calmed my nerves. He had a feminine gentleness which I found hard to reconcile with being a chess master. I sensed curiosity in his eyes, but no distrust, or perhaps I just preferred not to see it.

I walked along the path behind him and pondered my opening gambit. A brown hare in the grass wiggled its ears and hopped off. We followed it with our eyes. I could not imagine Rausis shooting a hare for his dinner roast.

– He's out early today, Rausis said.

– His tail makes me think of chess, white underneath and black on top, I said.

– We meet every night, Rausis said.

There was a metal step in front of the door. I wiped my shoes on it and stepped inside hesitantly.

– Greetings from Jouni Yrjölä.

– Thank you, it was an honour to play him.

– I hear you beat him twice in Finland.

– I got lucky.

– Lucky?

– The games could have gone either way.

Rausis closed the door, pulled out one of the plastic chairs, hung up his stick and said he used it as a precaution since he had suddenly lost the feeling in his legs a couple of times. Now he was fit and taking walks every day.

He moved his chair to avoid the last rays of the sun, which were blinding him. For a moment, he sized me up with his eyes.

– Did Jouni mention Strasbourg? he asked.

– In passing. Said he'd wondered how you'd been doing since.

– If it hadn't been for that tournament, I'd be dead already, Rausis said as if he was talking about the weather.

I was startled, and wanted to ask him about it, but could not find the right words. Then I thought it might be a sensitive topic, and it would be better to return to it later.

I handed him my gift, the German translation of a photo book telling the story of my moped ride through Finland. He asked me to sign it. Leafing through the book, he came across a photo of the Manhattan skyline at night taped on the wall of an outdoor toilet.

– The twin towers of the World Trade Center were still there, I said.

– Bobby Fischer wept for joy when they collapsed, Rausis said.

– Yup, chess smarts are no guarantee of a sound mind, I said.

I hung my jacket on a wall hook. On the table were a laptop computer, a mobile phone, a bunch of keys, a pretty sugar dish and a plastic box containing salami sandwiches. An orange vest, a woollen jumper, a peaked cap and an umbrella hung on wall hooks. The walls of the shack were faux wood laminate. A bare light bulb was suspended from the ceiling. A Pirelli calendar would not have looked out of place on the wall. One such calendar adorned Kafka's former office in Prague.

A transistor radio was playing Schumann's Piano Concerto. Igors turned it off, saying that Spidola was one of the best products of Soviet Latvia's electronics industry. The telescopic aerial had jammed, the carry handle was broken, and the device crackled a bit, but otherwise it worked fine.

Igors read a text message on his mobile phone. No doubt he had mentioned the Strasbourg incident to remind me that it was the real reason for my being there, even though I had not had the guts to say so. The idea that he had avoided death thanks to the incident sounded far-fetched. Perhaps he felt the need to account for the reasons that led up to it when he agreed to give the interview I had read in a chess magazine.

I told him about playing chess in Vērmanes Park and how friendly the other players had been. After only a few games, I felt that I belonged among them. This hardly would have happened if I had not spoken Russian. I had learned the rudiments of the language from my grandfather as a child.

– Gustav knew that you work here, I said. Someone told him.

– We met at the hospital, Igors said.

– So he told me. He also said you're a friendly guy.

– Gustav is the little big man of Russian literature, Igors said. Quite a character.

– Have you played him?

Igors said he had not had the time. Now he had time, but beating an amateur would be unfair and uninteresting. Occasionally he went for a walk in the park and watched the games without commenting. He had talked to Gustav a few times there.

He put the kettle on and said he was sorry the family samovar had been left in Sevastopol, where he had spent his youth. He had a spare mug in the shack in case someone happened to drop in. This was the first time that anyone had.

The text on the mug said *Keep calm and drink tea*. That would have been an appropriate motto for Rausis himself. He took a box of teabags off the shelf and made space for them on the table.

He was grey-bearded and thin, perhaps wasted by illness. He did not wear fancy clothes; why should he? He was good-humoured and appeared to be content with his life. I am certain that he was not merely pretending to be happy, American style. I imagined that I had learned with age to distinguish what was relevant about my fellow human beings. Their handshake told me a great deal, and the rest was revealed by their bookshelves. It was extremely rare for me to reverse my first impression.

The lights went on in one of the apartments in the house under construction. Igors said a workman was putting the finishing touches to it and would bring him the keys. Within six months, the house would be filled with well-to-do families and the parking lot with their expensive cars. The people of Riga were prepared to forgo everything else for a good car. Space would be left for vegetable patches, but it would probably remain empty.

– The car seems to be king in Riga, I said.

– So it is, unfortunately, Igors said.

He poured steaming water into the mugs, handed me a teabag and said he was working the shift from 6 pm to 8 am. He had to tour the site every two hours. There was no bed in the shack, but that did not matter, since he was not allowed to sleep. He could think as much as he pleased. He could spend all night reading, playing internet chess or watching films on his computer screen. He was paid five euros an hour. When asked why he wanted to do this work, he had said "to get rich".

– No fear of robbers, I suppose, I said.

– The only thing moving here at night is that hare.

– Do you still work as a chess coach?

Igors said the Latvian federation had allowed him to continue to teach at a children's chess school, for which he was duly grateful. It kept him in touch with life.

– When do you sleep?

– Wherever and whenever I can: on the tram, for example. That was very handy on tournament trips.

– And where do you live? I asked, just to make conversation.

He told me he lived with his wife Ajgul in the oldest building in Riga, which was originally a bank. They had a rented flat measuring just fifteen square metres on the second floor, which could be reached by lift. They had previously owned a four-room flat, but he had sold it to buy two smaller ones that he had given to his first wife Olita and their two daughters. Ajgul and Olita had later become friends.

Ajgul was from Kazakhstan. Her name meant "moon flower", which described her well according to Igors. She had a PhD in classical German literature and had taught at the University of Bonn. She could not find work in her field in Riga, since she spoke Latvian only passably. The country had very strict language requirements.

– Where are you staying? Igors asked.

– At the Hotel Monika, for a week.

– It has a free sauna.

– But no lake.

– During the tournament in Jyväskylä, we bathed in a sauna on the lakeshore. That was the highlight of the whole trip.

There was nothing related to chess in the shack. I knew that chess had filled his life for over forty years. He had four years left of his six-year ban.

– What has chess meant to you? I asked.

– A gateway to the world, to new countries and experiences.

He had realized what a privilege it was to be able to travel when he read about famous compatriots who had never been allowed outside the Soviet Union. One sad example was Mikhail Bulgakov, who was born in Kyiv. Paris and the freedom it stood for were an important symbol in Bulgakov's works. He was bitter about never having been permitted to go there. On the other hand, the poet Joseph Brodsky, another writer who was important to Igors, had been expelled from his country.

Igors said that there were people living under the yoke of the Kremlin who had never felt their lack of freedom. Their ingenuousness had made them free.

– Alexander Pushkin was never allowed to leave Russia either, I said.

– Pushkin was at loggerheads with the authorities, Igors said.

– That's what you get, every time.

I told him about a German friend of mine who had studied French in Moscow. For him, too, Paris was the shining city of dreams and would remain forever out of reach. When the Berlin Wall collapsed, he obtained a passport, but he was broke and still unable to travel. The dream turned into an open sore. His drinking habit did not help. He said anyone who was capable of talking about life in East Berlin in the 1980s had never experienced it.

Igors said he was grateful for everything his country had done for him. He considered himself a Russian patriot and believed in the socialist ideals of equality and a good life. He had inherited this attitude from his childhood home. In the Soviet Union, no one had to live in the street or worry about where the next meal was coming from. The spiritual side of life was more important than conspicuous consumption. People read good books and discussed them with friends and family. It was a pity that Gorbachev had allowed the Soviet Union to collapse. The hammer and sickle had been replaced by the McDonald's logo, and freedom of speech had brought American TV shows and porn.

– That's a pretty ideal, I said.

I believed there was some truth to Igors's description, but thought it best not to bring up the dark side of the Soviet Union, or his own privileges, let alone the collapse of the Soviet state, which I considered a stroke of good fortune for mankind. Nor did I wish to stoop to complaisance.

– Where did you start your conquest of the world?

Igors told me his father had taught seamen to operate a fishing boat in Alexandria, where the whole family had moved. Igors learned Arabic at the age of five and served as his parents' interpreter in shops and in other practical situations. The experience boosted his self-confidence.

Their home street was lined with cafés and coffee shops. He remembered the chatter, the clinking of cups and spoons and the aroma of roasted coffee beans like yesterday. The street was a scene from the Thousand and One Nights.

When Israel attacked Egypt, they had to return post haste to Sevastopol. Igors still went there once a year to visit his parents' grave. In his dreams, he returned to Sevastopol almost nightly, heard the murmur of the sea and relived his happy childhood. Sevastopol and its sea views were his patrimony and his lifeblood. He thought it was not possible to become so strongly attached to any memory without having formed an emotional bond with it in childhood.

With its cypresses and palms, the Crimean Peninsula was Russia's subtropical region exalted by poets. Pushkin painted a fairytale picture of it in his poetry. Igors said that if he had made a career as a doctor, he would have settled permanently in Sevastopol, but living there would have been difficult for a chess trainer and professional. Moreover, many Ukrainians despised him for having been born in Lugansk, the country's easternmost corner.

– What does the Ukrainian way of life mean to you? I asked.

– You have to sleep, eat and drink well, and tell jokes.

– Sounds simple.

– Understanding simple things is often hardest of all.

Igors said he would like to show me the fantasy city of his dreams. Because of his illness, Ajgul would not let him travel alone. There were no direct flights from Riga or Berlin to Sevastopol, but it could be reached without any problem via Moscow, and obtaining a visa was not expensive.

– Have you ever been to Ukraine?

– Once, to Odessa. But then Russia occupied Crimea.

– That made life better for the Crimeans, Igors said and wedged the window open.

I did not reply to this either, although I wanted to. I would never have dreamed of visiting the region after the invasion. The occupation had eroded my pacifism, but not badly enough to take out the army rifle my grandfather had hidden in the foundations of our summer cottage.

Aside from the Russian issue, on a human level I felt at home in Igors's company. The situation was similar to that with my friend Daniel. Igors and Daniel would have been on the same political wavelength, whereas I tended to agree with the politics of Daniel's late father.

It was as if Igors and I had known each other for ages. Nonetheless, I was surprised when he invited me to travel with him to Sevastopol.

– Did you start playing as a child? I asked to change the subject.

– I didn't start until I was fourteen.

Igors suspected that his late start may have been the reason why he never made it to the absolute top. He played his first open tournament in Sevastopol around the age of fourteen. He started by losing several games, only achieving a draw in one. The same thing happened to another player, and eventually they played one another.

The game lasted more than six hours. His opponent was over ninety years old. He was exhausted, and tears started running down his cheeks. In an equal position in the endgame, the old man's eyes turned to the sea view, dyed red by the setting sun, and he tipped his king to resign.

Igors said that when he played his last game in his last tournament in Strasbourg, he was in a medically-induced stupor and wept. These two incidents framed his adventures in the world of competitive chess.

Igors had been diagnosed with kidney cancer twenty years earlier. It metastasized to a brain tumour that the doctors did not dare operate, as this could have resulted in the loss of speech, perhaps even of eyesight. He was given only a few years to live, but the doctor who made the diagnosis broke his promise and died first.

– As long as I want to stay alive, the whitecoats are powerless, Igors said.

Igors's mobile phone clicked. He answered in Latvian, which sounded like no other language I had ever heard. When the conversation was over, he said his daughter had called to ask him how he was. They talked daily.

When he heard that I was not familiar with Riga, Igors told me about the city's sights and museums. They did not interest me, but to be polite I opened the city map and drew circles around the places he recommended.

The first time I went to Rome, I rushed through the obligatory sights. Once I was done with them, I was free to lounge around in parks and cafés.

Igors spoke German fluently, so we alternated between German, English and occasionally Russian, depending on the topic. Since we had different mother tongues, misunderstandings and distorted shades of meaning were always a potential problem. Nonetheless, I was confident that I would understand the essential message.

– I'll pay a visit to the privy in the yard, I said.

– There's no water there. You can go to the bathroom on the construction site.

– The outhouse will do fine. I built one in my backyard in Finland, I said and went out.

Outdoor privies were the subject of my first book. When I held a freshly printed copy in my hands, I thought that even if I achieved nothing else in my miserable life, this illustrated book would shine as a beacon in the sea of literature. My reputation as a crap author preceded me to Germany when *Die Zeit* published some of my photographs of outhouses in a lifestyle article.

From the door of the plastic loo, I glimpsed distant cottonwool clouds dyed by the setting sun. In a time-honoured sequence, the sun slowly vanished from view and the stars came out. One day less to go.

The grassy meadow in the background was overgrown with cow parsley. Why is the plant also called "mother-die"? "Wild chervil" sounds better.

To pass the time, Igors could turn this meadow into a potato patch and bring in a few summer chickens which would have plenty of forage. The area would become prettier, even though it would never turn into the Garden of Eden. To be sure, I had no idea whether he still had the strength to work the land.

From time to time in Berlin, I had missed my former career as a gardener and chicken farmer, when success was in my own hands. Now I tended the garden of the mind. My visiting card said I was the manager of a small chicken farm. After leaving the bank, I did not have the temerity to call myself a photographer or author. By that time, I no longer felt the need to pretend that I was in my right mind.

Igors had turned on the light in the shack. He poured boiling water in our mugs and showed me a postcard, a view of Sevastopol. He had studied medicine there to become a surgeon. His student dorm was furnished with bunk beds, and life was pretty chaotic, including at night. He married a fellow student so that they could get a room of their own. The marriage was dissolved amicably just before they graduated.

Igors told me he used to go diving and harpooning fish near Sevastopol. Once he hit a stingray before realizing what an enormous specimen it was. Its thorntail pierced his right arm, and his wetsuit filled with blood. A man who happened to be riding his sidecar motorcycle on the beach saved Igors's life by taking him to hospital.

The accident was a reminder of life's unpredictability. It changed his perception of the sea, but did not make him fear it.

For a long time, he was unable to use his arm, and his fore-finger was damaged permanently. He had to give up his dream of becoming a surgeon. He could not fire a rifle, but that was not important. He showed me the long scar on his arm.

– It was my own fault for killing a living creature.

– Jesus chose fishermen as his disciples, I said. What kind of fisherman is one who catches nothing?

– True, my dad was the captain of a fishing boat.

– I've loved angling ever since I was a kid. I never thought of it as killing.

I told him of Marie, who lived next door to me in Berlin. She had a similar scar on her forearm. She told me it came from the inmate number tattooed there at Sachsenhausen concentration camp. Her parents had already been murdered by then. After the war, her foster mother wanted to have the tattoo removed and told friends the scar was caused by an incendiary bomb. When Marie showed me the scar, her eyes told me the rest, which she did not wish to discuss any further.

Igors told me the story of a Russian grandmaster who played chess with the commander of a concentration camp. After losing five games in a row, the commander placed his pistol on the table. Undeterred, the prisoner won the sixth game as well. Instead of shooting him, the commander moved him to a section of the camp where living conditions were better, and the grandmaster survived to tell the tale.

I said I had heard you can get along in an ordinary prison once you learn the ropes. It was best not to beat a lifer at checkers.

In Crimea as a little boy, Igors had seen traces of the horrors perpetrated by the Nazis: ruined houses, horse skeletons, human remains, wrecked military equipment. He had imagined the skulls with living hair and skin on them. These horrors had invaded his dreams, and it had taken some time for him to exorcise them. Perhaps they were still haunting him in some hidden corner of his mind.

I told him I had been intending to visit the Riga Ghetto Museum, but had wound up in the Botanical Gardens instead, where I had watched exotic butterflies flitting about in a tropical hothouse. I had returned to the Hotel Monika light of step and heart.

In the villages of eastern Germany, I had seen memorials containing the names of soldiers killed in the First World War, but none with the names of the victims of the Second World War, although apparently there had been a few. The GDR had washed its hands of the sins of the Nazis.

Igors said that around the time when Hitler came into power, Stalin destroyed Ukraine's agricultural sector and caused a famine that killed millions. The country's intelligentsia were also eliminated. Uncle Joe sent Ukrainian soldiers to the worst spots during the Winter War against Finland in 1939. Probably most of them were killed. It did not bother Stalin to send soldier boys to their death; the females could always give birth to new ones. Igors knew the "Shots of Mainila" that started the Winter War, and which Stalin claimed had been fired by the Finns, had actually been fired from the Soviet side. As for Otto Wille Kuusinen and his puppet regime set up by Stalin, Igors considered them traitors.

– Let Otto enjoy his laurels in the Kremlin Wall, I said.

His injured arm did not prevent Igors from working on call at an emergency clinic. He said there were only a few emergencies per day, and he would play chess with an ambulance driver for hours. By that time, he had already won a few minor tournaments.

In his work, Igors became familiar with death. When he was taking a severely injured man to hospital, the patient anxiously asked the surgeon whether he would survive. "Is life really that important?", the surgeon replied. "It will end one day." Probably nowhere but in Russia could a doctor say such a thing in a way that the patient understood as comforting. This surgeon applied natural methods in his practice: if patients die, they die; if they recover, they do so of their own accord.

Igors left Crimea after he met Olita at a chess tournament. They were married, and Igors moved in with her in Riga. He adopted her surname and added the letter 's' to his first name.

Igors then applied for a grant to do a PhD in sports medicine at the University of Tartu. If he had obtained it, he would have moved to Estonia, and chess might have remained just a hobby for him. However, his application was turned down, and he had to find a job. To be licenced to practice medicine in Riga, he would have had to study for another two years, which he was not inclined to do.

Olita played chess professionally on the army team. She was paid a decent salary as well as travel, board and lodging during tournaments. The army uniform was another perk. She had already won the Latvian women's championship.

At Igors's request, Olita introduced him to the army officials in charge of the chess team, who offered him a job coaching juniors. Ukrainian chess players had an excellent reputation. His coaching abilities were appreciated, and he was sent to the Moscow Chess Academy, by far the most prestigious institution in the field.

That was the end of Igors's involvement with medicine. He said he thought it was better to have wasted six years than to spend his whole life practising a profession that did not really appeal to him in the way that chess did. His mother was unhappy because he had dashed her high hopes for him. She was a physician and served as the vice-principal of a medical university. For her generation, chess was a strange choice of profession. She would have to swallow her disappointment, however; many a life had been ruined by trying to live up to parental expectations.

I said my mother did not shout for joy either when I left the bank – before it could leave me. I fashioned a rosette on my felt hat from a tie I had worn at the bank. The tie was a gift from my mother and a hint to stop yobbing about, which was something she had had to witness powerlessly. At the bank, I kept the tie in a desk drawer in case there were foreign visitors. The tie became collateral damage in the cycle of life.

At school, I once won a prize for a short story I had written. My mother was proud of the achievement, but said she hoped I would not become a writer. She was not joking. I know several male authors who have confessed to me on a sauna bench that the first time they felt free was standing next to their mother's grave – and not completely free even then. Sometimes I myself still felt my mother's well-meaning hands wielding puppet strings from beyond the grave.

Igors said he had met his current wife Ajgul in Paris. Igors's mother disapproved of her son living in Bonn with Ajgul while still married to Olita. Igors himself felt guilty about it. The Russians say a man must repeat the same mistakes three times to understand life.

In Bonn, Igors initially freeloaded off Ajgul, until he gained the right to take part in the Bundesliga team competition, in which he quickly began to earn sizeable sums.

A couple of years later, Igors persuaded Ajgul to quit her job as lecturer at the University of Bonn and to move to Riga. Igors said it was customary for a Muslim woman to follow her husband, who in this case was a selfish bastard.

Igors set off on his scheduled round. I pondered how random events can spin the wheel of life into a new position, or bring it to a sudden end. If that biker had not turned up with his sidecar, Igors might not have been alive anymore, nor would I have been sitting here, poking around in his life.

Igors returned to the shack, hung his stick on a hook and said that when the Soviet Union collapsed, funding for chess also dried up, and the teachers at the academy were left destitute. That was when he understood that money had a value. The privilege of being allowed to travel abroad lost its lustre once the gates were thrown wide open for everyone.

He had to look for work elsewhere. He worked short stints as a chess coach until the Bangladesh chess federation offered him a post as coach of their national team. This work continued off and on for almost a decade. The players were particularly motivated and hardworking. Several members of the team became grand-masters, and two women also attained a high level of proficiency. He was particularly pleased by this, although it was not all his doing.

Dhaka, the capital of Bangladesh, had 16 million inhabitants according to official statistics, but the true figure was much higher. However, no one knew for sure: people came and went, living in the streets, the vegetable seller in her cart, the taxi driver in his car and many with nothing but a cardboard box for shelter.

Household waste, sewage and toxic industrial effluents all went straight into the River Buriganga. The water was black, stink-ing jelly, in which no living organism could survive except for one species of fish, which was eaten as a great delicacy.

When he visited a textile mill and saw the conditions that people worked in there, he broke into tears. The inhabitants were poor as church mice and their homes collapsed of their own accord. Back in the 17th century, Dhaka had been the richest city in the Mughal Empire.

Despite the poverty, Igors said he only encountered smiles in Bangladesh, none of the familiar Western morosity. Practitioners of six different religions lived peacefully side by side. Only once did he see someone cry, when a man was flogged for stealing a chicken.

After Bangladesh, he coached chess players in Iran, Iraq, Morocco and Tunisia. He liked the Arab world, even though he was originally a *Homo sovieticus* who worshipped the Central Committee of the Communist Party rather than God.

The minarets' calls to prayer had already made an impression on him in Crimea, where he knew some Muslim Tatars. Ajgul, too, was a Muslim who prayed daily and read the Qur'an.

Igors's childhood years in Egypt, when he had learned Arabic, helped him get along in these countries, although spoken Arabic differed from one country to the next, and some dialects were mutually unintelligible. On returning to Egypt as a coach, he discovered that mass tourism had brought corruption, which was rare in the Alexandria of his childhood. Foreigners were now continually being pestered for a gift.

In his experience, there was no corruption in Iran. In Tunisia, he occasionally had problems with the bureaucracy because his French was not good enough. He had learned nine languages, seven of which he spoke fluently. The Latin he had learned at university in Sevastopol as part of his medical studies helped him learn other languages, but he felt he was not fully present when speaking a foreign language. However, the language of chess was and still is universal.

Exotic foods were always available, and the range of spices and fruit was incredible. He started his mornings with coffee, bread, cheese and marmalade. After a game, a glass of rosewater calmed him down. The blood oranges in Tunisia were unimaginably sweet. The shops in Soviet Latvia carried spotty apples; at Christmas time, if you were lucky, you might find tangerines; fishmongers mainly sold tinned fish.

Igors put a box of chocolates on the table and told me to have some. He said Ajgul had packed it in his bag. The box read "Riga Black Balsam since 1752".

– How about the relationship between Islam and chess? I asked.

He said the problem was that the game was confused with gambling, which was forbidden. In Ancient Egypt, chess pieces were burned and players were whipped. In the old days, the Orthodox Church of Russia had also banned chess.

And yet the game had continued to be played at all times. In the Abbasid period, when receiving religious scholars, the Caliph of Baghdad covered his chessboard with a cloth.

The Grand Mufti of Saudi-Arabia banned chess, appealing to the Qur'an. In Iran, Ayatollah Khomeini reversed the ban on chess in the late 1980s on condition that it was not played for money. Some other Islamic countries also began to adopt a more relaxed attitude, although a certain influential Turkish imam quite recently called playing chess a sin worse than eating pork.

William Burroughs asserted that chess had been invented by Arabs: "Nobody can sit like an Arab. The classical Arab chess game was simply a sitting contest. When both contestants starved to death it was a stalemate."

According to Igors, what writers said about chess tended to be fiction. Chess probably originated in India, whence it spread to the Islamic world following the Arab conquest of Persia. The Arabs and Persians also developed the art of chess problems.

After his stint in the Arab world, Igors continued his chess career as a coach and player in the Czech Republic, near the German border, where he and Ajgul lived for several years. Ajgul already spoke Czech before they moved there.

A sudden downpour rattled on the roof. Rain streamed down the windows. Nature says thank you, Igors said. The mist softened the contours of the surrounding buildings, which had no life or stories to tell. Once people started moving in, he would have to seek a new job. Seek and ye shall find.

Teaching children was now his last remaining link with chess. Because of his illness, Igors depended on Ajgul. He could use public transport for free, as could Ajgul as his carer.

– How do you feel about your illness?

As a doctor, he said he understood it better than laypeople would, but he was suspicious of the omniscient and mechanistic view of human health that prevailed in academic medicine.

He was familiar with Louise Hay's ideas about the psycho-somatic origin of diseases. According to Hay, our thoughts and attitudes have a major impact on our health. People must accept themselves and their illnesses. Destructive thoughts can cause illnesses or aggravate them, and thus impede healing.

His illness had gradually become like a close friend, adding depth to his life. Igors lived peacefully in its company, and had no wish to lie on a psychiatrist's sofa, plumbing the depths of his subconscious. We all have the tendency to foist the responsibility for our existential problems on priests, doctors and psychologists instead of confronting them head-on and accepting mortality.

Igors had a good wife, two children and two grandchildren. When the Grim Reaper arrived, Igors would doff his hat to him.

– That sounds rather like what a Turkish taxi driver said in Berlin.

– Fight, and you may lose. Don't fight, and you've already lost, Igors said.

– But yesterday's losers are not today's winners, as Brecht wrote in his sermonising style.

Igors said that no amount of philosophy or fighting can save you from the finiteness of life. In the West, death is hidden and reduced to a funeral service, narrowing our emotional life and increasing our terror of the end. At the same time, this attitude reveals a fear of life, for the art of living and the art of dying are ultimately the same thing. Fear can only be overcome by looking it straight in the eye.

When teaching chess in Islamic countries, he had learned that God's friends need not fear the end. A situation such as his might be sad, but it was not comfortless.

I said I had pondered the same theme when writing my book on the old cemeteries of Helsinki. I began to understand people who saw cemeteries as pilgrimage sites and God's fields in which the seeds of the new germinate. Death was not present there in the same way as in the forests killed by human activity that I had photographed in the border region between Czechoslovakia and the GDR.

Cemeteries had become dumb; new headstones no longer bore epitaphs, and the ancient religious symbols were also on the way out. I considered suitcase-shaped headstones to be inadvertent metaphors for the final journey and travesties of the ideal of equality.

An acquaintance of mine had carved a headstone for his mother out of the barn doorstep on which she used to sit. The beautiful moss-covered stone celebrated life. The abodes of the dead are mirror images of those of the living. In this respect, as in others, I was yesterday's man.

I said I had learned a natural attitude to death from my Orthodox heritage. In East Karelia, I had seen mourners taking leave of the deceased. The body lay in an open coffin for everyone to see, children included. This was how it was done in Finland, too, in the old days.

I told Igors about my melanoma. It had never occurred to me to befriend my cancer. Perhaps I had learned to tolerate it, like an old couple who no longer had anything to say to one another, but felt obliged to stay together. This wisdom would be sorely tested as I approached the final frontier.

– Don't be afraid. It won't help you, Igors said.

– I know…

– There's more light in the world than you can see from the window.

My godmother lived to be a hundred years old, and suspected that God had forgotten to collect her. Soon after her birthday, however, God disproved her theory. The officiating pastor was told this story before the funeral. At the funeral service, he spoke about the "tragedy that had suddenly struck the family". If he had been told that my godmother's favourite tree was the birch, he would have talked about "whispering fir trees". Such ministers made the Lutheran Church a dismal place.

A Russian friend living in Helsinki told me that at his father's funeral reception, the mourners ate, drank and sang his father's favourite songs. The deceased was also offered a dram. When taking a post-mortem photograph, the photographer told the subject to lie still for a moment. According to my friend, that funeral was more fun than a Finnish wedding.

– Sounds like the right spirit, Igors said.

At the funerals of Igors's parents, the mourners had left a plateful of strawberry *kissel* for the deceased, giving the soul of the departed the pleasure of being served dessert.

I said Finnish funerals could also be more relaxed sometimes, but that required liquor. Pentti, an honorary member of a literary crowd I was part of, had been cremated. We picked up the urn and took it for a pub crawl. We had our first shots at Pentti's regular haunt and placed the urn on a chair. The waiter was in tears; she had known him for years. We thought Pentti would also like to visit some other watering holes and pressed on, but left the urn at the coat check. When the last restaurant closed, we realized Pentti was missing. I pointed out that every one of us would be left by the wayside in turn.

Igors said an Algerian chess colleague had told him about Albert Camus's mother, who was illiterate. When anyone she had been close to died, she said "there's another one that's stopped farting". She did not shed a tear when she heard her son had died in a car accident. In Camus's novel *The Stranger*, the protagonist was accused not only of murder, but also of not having wept at his mother's funeral.

Camus's father had been killed by the Nazis. Igors suspected that the mother had been hardened by the family's sufferings, or else she considered death to be so natural that there was no point making a fuss about it.

I had read that as a child Camus played goalkeeper because his mother could not afford to buy him football shoes. He said he had learned everything essential about life from football. I recalled that some grandmaster had said something similar about chess. According to Camus, it was only possible to lead a morally defensible life by establishing strict rules and living by them.

I was tired, so I asked when the next bus was leaving for the city centre. Igors checked the timetable and discovered that the last bus had already gone. He invited me to visit his monastic cell again the following evening.

– Perhaps we can have a game tomorrow before it gets too late, I said.

– OK, I'll bring a chess set.

– I want to experience a real master's touch once in my life.

– I've gone downhill.

– Hardly far enough…

We said goodbye at the gate. The rain had stopped, but the trees were still dripping. I tried to avoid the puddles on the path. At my age, I no longer felt like splashing straight across. The reflection of street lights on the water surface still gave me a thrill. It would be a little death not to notice them.

The street was silent, as if time had stopped. The pavement gleamed in the pale moonlight. Another early summer day tailing away into darkness. I forced myself to think I should be grateful for this unique moment, and to endow it with meaning. A walk to the hotel was more appropriate for my mood than a bus ride.

Perhaps Igors had taken my comment on the importance Camus attached to following the rules as a hidden barb. How was it possible that, even at death's door, Igors appeared to embody an untroubled affirmation of life? Perhaps he did not give any thought to such doors. His faith must have given him the strength to reject alienation. He believed in the victory of the imperishable.

I was reminded of the Swedish poet Gunnar Ekelöf. During his last illness, Ekelöf had suffered agonies which could not be allayed by pills. Ekelöf wrote that pain was part of human life. He incorporated pain in his poems and entertained it from morning to night. He thought of himself as a resistance fighter chafing against death with words. He and Igors were kindred spirits.

I had read about a man who only began to think that his life was meaningful when he fell seriously ill. When healthy, he had never been able to rid himself of the sense of not having made enough of his life. Was he just clinging to a fiction?

After ending his professional career, former world champion Anatoly Karpov played some exhibition games in Finland. He turned in a routine performance: he could use the money. After the games, he seemed restless and wore an expression of melancholy reminiscent of a wolfhound parked in front of a shop. Then again, he had always looked like a humourless party official, stalwart of a barren system.

Igors had already survived twice as long as the doctor had predicted. If his attitude had been stiflingly joyless, he might already have been dead. I assumed that he had also reached a truce with his previously diagnosed kidney cancer. His body language strengthened the impression of hopefulness.

If only I could be as calm and hopeful as Igors about my illness, and still enjoy a game of darts and cooking pancakes on an open fire afterwards. The glare of the blaze would replicate similar moments from my childhood and later years.

Igors had mentioned the Strasbourg incident. I had not had the nerve to take him up on it; perhaps tomorrow I would have the courage to do so. It would also be nice to meet Ajgul and hear her version of events and her opinion of her husband, but preferably when he was not present.

Evidently Igors had never experienced feelings of homelessness and transience when living in various parts of the world. It was said that such feelings undermined your psychological equilibrium. He could hardly have taken his favourite objects with him, if he had even had such possessions.

The idea of leaving everything I knew and spending the rest of my life in some new city seemed impossible. A completely unfamiliar place would hardly dispel the fear of death. I would not have time to learn a new language, nor would I even wish to do so. I still hope to improve my German, and will probably speak it best when on my deathbed.

Some of my friends had moved to a new country to escape emotional issues. Those issues, however, clung to them like burdocks. Although they had left some of their everyday obligations behind, these were replaced by new obligations, many of them more burdensome than the old ones. A person often meets his destiny on the road he took to avoid it.

A fellow student of mine travelled from one continent to the next. In the end, he realized that he could have discovered his truth just as surely in a good novel. He was left with hundreds of photographs that showed where he had travelled but were devoid of rousing emotional experiences.

As for Igors, travelling the world had been his daily bread and butter. Now he seemed to be living on his memories. If he had any shadow of a doubt or a hidden dark side, he did not reveal it. Perhaps that would have required a toothbrush mug of vodka, which he never drank.

I had already decided that I would only leave Berlin in a coffin or in chains. The thought was soothing, and my illness would hardly weaken my resolve, although it might deprive me of my say in the matter. Inshallah, I thought, like Igors.

After lunch, I went to the park to watch the games. I immediately felt at home. There were some new faces, but no one looked like a tourist. Either the chess tradition had never made it to the city's brochures, or the tourists had something better to do.

I shook hands with Gustav and told him about my visit to the building site.

– Igors looked well, I said.

– He's a tough cookie, Gustav said.

– What sort of man is he, in your opinion?

– A bit of a strange bird.

– How so?

– Believes in God, comforts other people, doesn't drink. But still cheats.

– Don't you ever cheat?

– Not in chess. Sometimes at cards, but not between friends.

– Why is no one playing at that granite table? I wondered.

Gustav said the chess players had asked the city to do something for them. The then mayor of Riga had had the table installed. For the same price, they could have had a long wooden table and an awning to keep off the rain. No one wanted to play at a single isolated table, but you could not expect the bigwigs to understand that. What Gustav would have liked was a spacious café where you could play in winter. There had been one just a stone's throw away;

its former owner was a chess player. Now the café had a new owner who wanted to make it a more lucrative business.

– That's the spirit of this capitalist time, Gustav said and sniffed. Even sport is wrecked.

– In the socialist countries, sport remained virtuous, I said.

– Well…when Olga, the Olympic hope of the weightlifting team, gave her rival Tanya a razor for her birthday, Tanya was furious and kicked Olga in the balls.

– Are you a sportsman?

– I played goalkeeper for FC Caramba Riga. Then I exchanged the ball for the bottle.

He said all he ever got from his club was his football shirt. A broken wrist had ended his career a quarter of a century earlier. It was set to end soon anyway, and without fanfare. His bravura was playing the accordion behind his back, but the injury made that difficult too. He ran his fingers along imaginary keys, hummed and said the tune was *Song to the Dnieper*.

I told Gustav I had played football in my student days on a team called Viva Zapata. Our red shirts sported the portrait of the grinning, walrus-whiskered freedom fighter Emiliano Zapata. Our team had more idealism than skill, but the joy of playing was the important thing.

– Did you ever play chess with Igors? I asked.

– No, nor tennis with Federer.

– Why do you think Igors cheated?

Gustav said Igors had been playing in small tournaments in recent years. He had been a good deal higher-rated than the other participants, and had picked up a lot of easy wins, but had only gained a few rating points. It was a laborious way to rise up the ranks. However, he was getting close to a 2 700 rating. Only one tournament victory more was needed, and that must have been his goal.

– It's a terrific rating, especially at his age, I said.

– Too high. Perhaps he thought he had nothing to lose.

– What if he'd made it? I asked.

– God only knows, but he won't say.

Gustav asked me to give Igors his regards if I met him again. They were born in the same year and, according to Gustav, had been hanging around for long enough.

– How long do you intend to cheat death? I asked.

– Until it mates me. When the game's over, the king and the pawns go back in the same box.

I shook his hand for goodbye and wished him a great endgame. Gustav returned to his table and lit a cigarette. He seemed to be as much a part of the park as the trees shading the tables.

Many players had set a round figure as their rating objective, and pursued that objective obsessively. My own objective was 2 000, which would have put me in the top one per cent of all the world's chess players. This would not be a problem as long as I remained a long way away, but it would be torture to end up just a couple of points short. This type of objective has nothing to do with reason. No doubt the momentary joy brought by attaining my goal would be replaced by a hollow feeling. Happiness keeps eluding us.

In chess circles, profession and social status were meaningless. Respect and pecking order depended on rating. At a certain chess café in Berlin, the owner always asked newcomers what their rating was. That was all he wanted to know.

Perhaps some sociology professor would develop a system to rate the social usefulness of individuals. The two ends of the scale could be 'essential' and 'insignificant'.

I walked along a boulevard lined by Art Nouveau buildings. When the thundering traffic began to feel stressful, I turned into a side street of run-down buildings and small shops, some of them boarded up.

An old-style clock with motionless hands protruded from a wall. It was exactly on time twice a day. Since I had left my office job, I had not had any use for an alarm clock. The summers were longer; I was in no hurry to get back from the ski trail. It was a luxury to be in control of one's own schedule.

Rainer Maria Rilke's novel *The Notebooks of Malte Laurids Brigge* tells the story of a man who has always been told that time is precious. He expects to live another fifty years and therefore thinks himself rich. Rather than changing his modest lifestyle, he decides to be thriftier than ever with his time. He gets up earlier, washes less elaborately and drinks his tea standing. He saves a little bit of time in everything. After a week, he realizes there are no savings to be found. He feels cheated.

He thinks there must be a time bank somewhere where he should be able to exchange at least a few of his measly seconds for money. He leafs through the phone book, but it is no use. Time is a touchy business for him, and as he thinks about it the earth moves under his feet. Lying in bed and slowly reciting poetry, he calms down.

Poetry had given solace to many people in a difficult pass, lighting up their murky existence. Perhaps I should rely on it now. If that time bank really existed, I would exchange my very last cents for time.

I came to a secluded park and sat down on a cast-iron bench warmed by the sun. A sparrow hopped about at my feet, but I had nothing for it to peck. It bounced around on two feet, took wing briefly, then hopped again. It needed to be fed by either the heavenly father or by some bird lover. My grandmother used to say that God had run out of colours when he created sparrows.

In China, Mao decided to exterminate all sparrows, considering them pests, and mobilized the people to kill them. This campaign, which was part of the Great Leap Forward, succeeded so well that the sparrow population was depleted to the verge of extinction. The crops were subsequently devoured by locusts and other insects, leading to a famine that killed tens of millions of people. China had to import hundreds of thousands of sparrows from the Soviet Union.

The gardener in charge of Hietaniemi cemetery always kept nuts in her coat pocket to feed squirrels. They recognized her and headed straight for her pockets. Once, finding nothing there, a squirrel bit her in the stomach. On hearing this story, the doctor at the first-aid clinic chuckled.

Once when I was a child, a squirrel climbed up my clothes in the hope of finding a nut. This was my first impression of a cemetery. I still remember the sensation of a bushy tail brushing my cheek.

On a cold winter's day, I sat shivering on the hillside next to the crematorium as horses pulled the gun carriage bearing the coffin of Mannerheim, the Marshal of Finland. Smoke puffed out of the crematorium chimney. To reassure me, I was told that Mannerheim would not be shoved into the oven.

Maple branches curved over me, vault-like, the wings of a guardian angel. The leaves, glittering in the backlight, quivered as they were caught in a breath of wind. White fuzz wafted in the air like snow.

Seeking comfort, I attached the winglike ala of a maple seed to my nose to celebrate this unique moment of grace. The tulips at the foot of the tree were already shedding their petals. Flowers could not be aware that they would bloom again next summer.

The sparrow had lost hope as far as I was concerned. If I were a sparrow, I would spend my time in the vicinity of a café. I would have to become accustomed to the hostility of humans if I did not observe table manners and content myself with pecking at crumbs on the ground. Conformists said let the rich get richer so there will be crumbs for the poor.

When my grandmother lay dying, she hoped that birds would accompany her across the border. She wanted her children to sprinkle breadcrumbs over her grave. The thought comforted her.

A pencil-thin old man shuffled along a sanded path, leaning on a pair of crutches. He wore a wide-brimmed hat, pale gloves and tie; perhaps he wished to convey a gentlemanly impression to the end. He was accompanied by a portly Labrador retriever whose walk was as laboured as that of his master. Perhaps the dog had eaten his master's food as well as his own.

No doubt this walk was a daily ritual for them. The old man stopped to sniff the white lilac blossoms, proving that he was still alive. The dog waited beside him. Which of them would be sent for first? The day when one of them kicked the bucket would be a sad one for the other.

That night, I received a text message. My Berlin friend Leo was in his final throes. This was no surprise. I first met Leo at a conference in Budapest in 1980. The subject was Hungary's economic reform. Participants lived in student dorms and dined together in the canteen. As a vegetarian, I scraped out the greasy bits of meat and gave them to the Romanian delegate sitting next to me. In return, he gave me potatoes, carrots and cabbage. It was a genuine win-win exchange in the spirit of brotherly love.

I played chess with Leo at the edge of the pool in the palatial Széchenyi thermal baths. Between games, he told me he was planning to write his doctoral thesis on the problems of the GDR economy. The problem was that the country had no problems. As we were riding on the back of swans in the amusement park merry-go-round, he invited me to visit him in Berlin.

In Berlin, we played our first game on the roof of his apartment building in Prenzlauer Berg. From there, we could see the phrase *Der Sozialismus siegt* (Socialism Will Win) on a neon sign that had been turned off to save electricity. During the game, the wind rose from the direction of the slaughterhouses in Friedrichshain, and we had to finish our game indoors. This was the first of my many visits to Berlin.

Having battered his head against the anti-fascist wall for quite some time, Leo eventually returned his party membership card to the Examination Committee. This act earned him the sack from the Academy of Sciences.

After reunification, his Moscow degree in Marxist economics was not worth the paper it was printed on, but he got a job as a property man and interpreter on a team shooting a documentary film on Kaliningrad. The documentary was shown at the Berlin Film Festival and garnered favourable reviews. As Leo and the team acknowledged their ovation on the podium, he thought he had finally discovered his purpose in life. I was happy for him, but envious at the same time. I was languishing under the yoke of the timecard, without any professional prospects, and with a long way to go before enjoying an unearned rest.

Leo was dropped from the team's next project. Apparently he had mixed up the production funding with his own finances. It also transpired that the reason for his expulsion from the Academy of Sciences was not political. His much-lauded final paper, on the strength of which he had been hired by the academy, turned out to have been plagiarized.

Leo's literary forays never gained any recognition, and he envied me my books. He drank what little money he had and treated me as an ATM machine, ruining our friendship.

He had told me he would make his exit quietly. He would get onto a train on the Trans-Siberian Railway, jump off somewhere near Lake Baikal, and walk off into the snowdrifts, letting the new snow falling cover his tracks. He would never see those snowdrifts now. Perhaps he would fly through the air on the back of a swan, escaping the crazy merry-go-round of our chaotic world.

A tortoiseshell butterfly flitted above the pansies in the park in meandering curves. It landed on a petal, then flew off again. It was a masterpiece of nature. Butterflies have a short life, although a few of them enjoy the dubious privilege of immortality, impaled on a pin in a glazed box.

The embalmed Lenin can be admired in his mausoleum on the Red Square. Vladimir was dead for only a brief moment, after which he continued to perform good deeds as a resurrected philanthropist, setting things right in the world.

I once found a common blue butterfly between the pages of a copy of Nikolai Gogol's *Dead Souls* borrowed from the library. I wondered whether the butterfly had been pressed on purpose. Perhaps someone reading the book had found it already dead and used it as a bookmark, or had simply wanted to gladden the next reader.

An invitation to a ball arranged by the Finnish–Soviet Society once fell out from between the pages of a manual on repairing mopeds. The date of the ball had passed, the Soviet Union had been buried and the society disbanded, whereas my grandfather moped was still going strong.

This park bench could have become a daily stop for me if I had lived in Riga. External routines had brought order and harmony into my life. I could determine my daily schedule freely, but my days were still subdivided by my habits, as they were for the sanatorium patients in Thomas Mann's novel *The Magic Mountain* and, indeed, for Mann himself.

If I were to be permanently hospitalized, the daily routines would be familiar, but I would not be free to break them, aggravating the horror of such a fate.

This bench was the only one in the vicinity, and it could not be reserved. Every day, I would have to worry that someone was already occupying it. Sharing it with a complete stranger did not tempt me any more than the small talk that would entail. In hospital, some other poor soul would be thrust by chance into the neighbouring bed and tied down to it. There would be no way to rid myself of a tiresome neighbour, and yet I would not have the heart to turn my back on them. In this respect, Igors and Gustav had been lucky.

As the pains get worse, terminal care is around the corner and the patient may be tempted to self-terminate. A fellow sufferer wished to dress up just once in his life. He hired a tailcoat from a costume rental company, put it on and jumped off a balcony in a tower block.

I leaned back, closed my eyes and listened to the dark song of a blackbird and the rustling of leaves. A breeze caressed my face. I imagined I was looking at crinkled leaves on the surface of a lake. The scent of bird cherry was intensified by the fact that I could not see the actual blossoming tree.

Back in my home park in Berlin, I had met an old man who talked to blackbirds. He would whistle in their direction, and the birds would reply. They would react to his call even in winter. He had learned as a child to imitate their flute-like song. The locals thought him mad. He himself thought *they* could not see or hear the things around them, which was the worst form of madness.

In a poem by Bertolt Brecht, a man wakes up in hospital, hears a blackbird singing, and ceases to fear death. He will not want for anything when he no longer exists. He rejoices at the thought that there will still be birdsong when he is gone.

It was too warm in the shack. I asked if I could leave the door open. I put a birchbark punnet of strawberries on the table. They smelled of… strawberries. The little basket reminded me of seeing a meadow red with wild strawberries in my childhood.

– There was no sign of the hare, I said.

– It'll turn up in an hour or two.

Igors put the kettle on. He told me he had taught at the chess school again today. The children trusted him and radiated enthusiasm and openness. They ranged from four-year-olds to schoolchildren. Only two of his couple dozen pupils were girls, and one of them had said she was quitting.

I said we would probably never see women playing chess in Vērmanes Park. In the Netflix miniseries *Queen's Gambit*, the heroine Beth is told that girls don't play chess. I heard that the series had induced many women to take up the game.

– How well do your youngest pupils understand chess?

– They know the moves, but they can't grasp the overall pattern on the board.

– José Raúl Capablanca was already an accomplished player at the age of four, I said.

– Well, he was the Mozart of chess.

– Does that mean they lost part of their childhood?

Igors did not see any problem with this. He said children play all sorts of games anyway, and you could see them sitting in front of flashing screens everywhere. When playing chess, children faced a living opponent and played with tangible pieces, which was better. He showed children moves and sequences with just a few pieces. It was just another kind of play, and the children loved it.

When a pawn that advanced to the eighth rank turned into a queen, it was like a fairytale miracle. Why did the knight move back and forth in such a strange way? And why was it allowed to leap over another piece, when a bishop was not? Igors explained that back in the 17th century bishops too could leap over other pieces, but that the rules were changed later.

The children learned that the aim of the game was to checkmate the opponent's king. He refrained from explaining the etymology of the word: the Persian word *mat* meant death. In most languages, the word for the position that ends the game is derived from the same root. The word *check* originally referred to the *shah*, i.e. the king.

I told him about a lady in Berlin who asked me to teach her ten-year-old daughter to play chess. She knew the moves, but that was about it. I told her what to aim for in the opening and what kind of moves to avoid. When we played, she made the very moves I had told her to avoid. She wanted to play, but she did not want to learn. In the TV series Beth, thirsting for knowledge even as a small child, is the exact opposite of this girl.

Igors said that children's enthusiasm for the game depended on their parents' support. Some parents – usually fathers – projected their own ambition onto their children, seeking to compensate for their own failures or frustrations. The same was true in all sport. However, one could not expect anyone to succeed if they did not have the fire in them.

When Igors's daughters played in a junior tournament in Sweden, one of the participants was the five-year-old Magnus

Carlsen. Magnus's father believed his son would become a champion, perhaps even world champion. The boy had an inexhaustible passion for chess. Watching him play, Igors realized that this passion came from within. Magnus already had the ability to concentrate and an incredible memory, both of which are essential qualities for chess players. Mikhail Tal was able to reproduce every game he had ever played.

I said I had been given my first chess set as a Christmas present in 1954. I still used the same set. Once when we moved house, the white king's crowned head came off and was lost. My father carved a new one; then, examining his work, commented that no one is perfect.

Once a white knight went missing, but I found it under the table I always sat at in the café I used to play in. After that, I always counted the pieces after the games to make sure none were lost. I would never have been able to find an identical replacement for love or money.

Samuel Reshevsky started playing chess at the age of four. I told Igors I had seen a photo of Reshevsky in Paris at the age of eight, playing a simultaneous exhibition against 20 dignified-looking gentlemen. The caption said he darted from one board to the next. One of the games was drawn; he won all the rest. In the photo, he wears the same kind of white sailor's suit that I had at his age. He did not go to school as a child, which led to his parents being sued in Manhattan Children's Court.

– I also had a suit like that, Igors said.

– In a class photo from my elementary school, I was the only child choked by a necktie.

Igors took out a bundle of black-and-white photographs. On top was a shot of him sitting between his parents. His father is wearing a ship captain's cap. In another picture, Igors sits on a rocky beach, sporting flippers and goggles. He had started diving before he went to school. In another photo, he is playing the violin. However, he stopped taking violin lessons early on.

Igors showed photos of himself playing chess in many different countries. In one, he had long hair like the Beatles, for which he was hassled by the police in Moscow. He kept a photograph of Karl Marx in his wallet, and told the police he had been inspired to grow his hair by the great man's example. He had his hair cut short when he started coaching in the Arab countries.

A colour photo showed Olita clasping a trophy she had received for winning the Latvian women's championship. She had a long row of these trophies on her bookshelf. Igors's grandfather posed for a photograph on the anniversary of the revolution with two rows of medals on his lapels; he looked like an iconostasis. He had fought in the Great War from the day it began until the fall of Berlin. He went to the grave wearing those medals.

On my iPad, I showed Igors a photo of a football match played on a muddy field during the trench warfare phase of the Finno–Russian War. My father stands in goal, his outfit consisting of boots, long underpants and a plain mesh T-shirt. The opposing team are playing shirtless. Behind the players is a lake in which the soldiers bathed and fished. My father also used a mesh shirt as a fishwell.

I had forgotten to show this photo to Gustav, who had also played goalkeeper. He had avoided military service by learning about neurological compulsions, which he pretended to be trying to cover up during the call-up examination. The chief officer of the conscription office had deplored that in Gustav the army had lost a strong soldier with the build needed to haul a field gun or to carry the flag in a parade.

Igors said the Latvian-born grandmaster Aron Nimzowitsch had managed to dodge the draft by claiming he had a fly in his head. In Israel, Nimzowitsch once played anonymously in a café.

Of course he won all his games. One of his opponents commented that he played in the style of Nimzowitsch.

I clicked up a photo from my student days that showed me standing in the lobby of the Helsinki School of Economics. On my feet were my grandfather's old ski boots which I claimed that I wore all year round, summer and winter. I carried my lecture notes in my grandmother's zippered shopping bag with rattan handles. A moth-eaten pullover completed my anti-consumerist look, and revealed my vanity.

The Helsinki Chess Olympiad in 1952 took place in the same institution, then a newly-completed architectural gem. The games were played in the assembly hall, which has a curving ceiling clad in Oregon pine that makes it look like a cathedral. The victorious Soviet team included legends such as Keres, Smyslov and Bronstein, all familiar names to me via their games. The Finnish team was headed by Eero Böök, whose chess manuals I knew through and through.

Igors ate a strawberry, praised its sweetness and said he had met Mr Böök once. He knew that the tournament in Kemeri, Latvia in 1937 had been a high point in Böök's career, as he defeated Reshevsky, the top US player, and drew with world champion Alexander Alekhine.

I said that once on a business trip to Paris, I skipped the afternoon meeting and wandered off to Montparnasse cemetery. While photographing the ornate headstones, I spotted the granite memorial to Alekhine. It was topped by a portrait of the world champion in relief, and in front of it was a chessboard. Someone had placed small stones on the board to mark the pieces, perhaps inspired by some childhood memory. The stone was engraved in gilt lettering: *Champion du Monde des Echecs*.

Igors said he had visited Alekhine's grave once during a tournament in Paris. The world was Alekhine's home, but he was never comfortable in it. During the Nazi occupation, he opportunistically wrote antisemitic articles, for which he was ostracized in the chess world. The Soviet Union considered him a bourgeois traitor. After Stalin died, however, Alekhine was elevated to the status of the greatest Russian player of all time.

Alekhine ruined his health with drink. Igors said this was the reason he lost the championship to the Dutchman Max Euwe in 1935. A few years later, Alekhine regained his title following a strict cure during which he only drank milk. He lived for chess alone, and played the game obsessively. Once another chess master took Alekhine and Capablanca to the theatre. Capablanca watched the play with unflinching concentration, whereas Alekhine barely raised his eyes from his magnetic pocket chess set.

During the last months of his life, Alekhine lived in a hotel in Portugal. He dozed in the hotel bar, hoping for someone to buy him a drink. As the end drew near, he asked to be taken to a night-club in order to see people around him one last time.

Alekhine died at his desk, a chessboard – his lifelong companion and the setting of glorious battles – within reach. He was the only world champion of chess in history to take his title to the grave with him.

Innumerable Russians have sunk into restless yearning and melancholy, seeking relief in alcohol. Finnish players were no strangers to Alekhine's kind of drinking either, as Igors said he had discovered at a party following a tournament in Jyväskylä. Igors himself was no drinker: he had only had one single shot of vodka in his life. Anatoly Karpov drank his first glass when he heard his coach had died.

I said that in Finnish male company, anyone who refused a drink was likely to be asked whether he was driving or on antibiotics. When friendship toasts were raised during Finno–Russian trade negotiations, only self-proclaimed teetotallers were allowed to abstain. Lashings of booze were used to winkle classified information out of the Finns.

Igors told me about a tournament he had played in Cádiz, Spain. One of the participants was a leading Finnish player, whose name he had forgotten. It was a windless day; the temperature approached fifty degrees centigrade. After consuming vast quantities of beer, the Finn wanted to go to the hotel sauna. The female porter told him it was only used in the winter. The Finn insisted: if he was not allowed to use the sauna, he would show his penis. And so he did. A photograph of the incident was published in the local newspaper, although the critical part was blacked out.

A bumblebee buzzed against the window pane, even though the door was open. Igors picked up a piece of paper and chased it out. He said he knew from experience that the shortest route might not lead anywhere, but a detour might teach you something. In Russia, any road that did not lead to a sanctuary was worthless. That was why there were so many detours, and why the main roads were in such poor repair.

Igors poured hot water in our mugs, took out a pair of tea bags and said no one had ever choked on tea in Russia. He snatched a sugar cube from a porcelain bowl. It was one of the few objects he had taken with him from his home in Sevastopol. He had admired its beauty as a child, and now it was the heart of his austere dacha.

I told him about a Russian friend of mine who used a tin can inherited from his mother as a flower pot. It once contained corned beef received from America in the final days of the siege of Leningrad. There were prettier souvenirs in the world, but this rusty, rectangular tin put my friend in mind of a hope that should never expire.

The friend in question told me his father had died of lung cancer. In hospital, his father had removed his oxygen mask to smoke a drag or two in secret. He had chosen to remain faithful to his passion to the very end. Gustav was equally loyal to his. He told me he smoked a couple of packs of cigarettes a day and drank vodka, even though he knew this was not good for his liver cirrhosis. He thought it healthy to eat a substantial amount of sausage before uncorking his vodka bottle. He suspected that he was enjoying his last summer of chess.

Igors said that every summer is somebody's last. Mikhail Botvinnik, who played seven world championship matches, said that each match shortened the players' life by one year. Botvinnik was born to a Russian Jewish family in the village of Kuokkala (today known as Repino) in the Grand Duchy of Finland.

Just preparing for such a match is exhausting, involving as it does endless move sequences, repetitions and analyses of the opponent's games. Many chess masters have in fact suffered breakdowns or become deranged in one way or another, which Igors did not consider to be coincidental. On the other hand, he said that no grandmaster ever contracted Alzheimer's, and they lived substantially longer than the population on average.

Igors felt that super-intelligent people were often in the worst danger of going astray; on the other hand, lack of talent provided no guarantee of a quiet life. Ultimately, what determines the course of a person's life is a mystery, as is why some people endure while others crack.

According to Igors, Bobby Fischer was the most talented player of all time, but his antics were incomprehensible. Fischer hated his native country and was a misogynist. Although he was half-Jewish, his last public appearances were marked by paranoid antisemitic bluster.

Fischer spent the last years of his life in Reykjavik, where he reputedly played chess on the internet. He had broken the long period of Soviet chess dominance in 1972, with the result that interest in the game shot up in the West, only to wane when Fischer withdrew from the chess arena. The downward trend was not reversed until Magnus Carlsen became world champion in 2013. Carlsen's impact was strengthened by his decision to start modelling for trendy clothes. He knew how to make money multiply.

Some people became addicted to chess, and it turned into a prison for them. The love of chess had left them no room for human love. Igors did not know a single grandmaster who led a harmonious family life.

Igors had also come across the theme of chess mania in literature. Zweig's *Chess Story* tells the story of Dr B, who is thrown in jail after Hitler's rise to power for hiding valuable objects owned by the aristocracy. In prison, he memorizes outstanding games from chess history from a book he has in his cell. He goes on to play against himself blindfold, dividing his mind into a "White Me" and a "Black Me", an absurd idea. The idea that Dr B should later defeat the world champion on a sea voyage though he has not touched a chess piece in twenty years is not plausible.

I pointed out that the story has little to do with chess. Moreover, the world champion is portrayed as a boorish lout. The plot is repetitive and the narrator prone to rationalized arguments, but the story does provide a reasonably credible portrayal of obsession. I preferred Nabokov's novel *The Luzhin Defence*, which provides a more realistic and nuanced depiction of chess. Here again, the protagonist goes insane. Both stories raise the same question: is chess just an innocent game, or does it attract madmen?

In Nabokov's novel, Luzhin thought that by moving a lime tree that grew on a hillside and looked like a knight he could capture a telegraph pole that had turned into a bishop. I said I experienced similar delusions as a child, until I instinctively realized I should distance myself from the game.

The cover of the German edition of Nabokov's novel depicted a little boy in front of a chessboard. I purchased the book just because of that picture. I recognized myself in that boy.

Igors said that Nabokov grew up in the Soviet Union, where chess had cult status and children would start playing when still in kindergarten. Even there, however, teachers understood that children should be children, and tried to keep the game as a formative play experience.

Comrade Lenin learned the game from chess books during his exile in Siberia. He had no one to play against. According to Igors, Zweig's story echoed this experience. Vladimir Ilyich became an accomplished chess player and sponsored chess in many ways. It was an effective form of mental gymnastics, used to bolster the reputation of the Soviet Union in the world and to prove the superiority of the communist system. The Bolsheviks treated the chessboard as a political battlefield.

Igors said that a certain etching made in 1909 had appeared on the market a decade or so ago. It allegedly shows Hitler and Lenin playing chess at the home of a Jewish family in Vienna. Hitler was in town at the time to try to sell his paintings, and Lenin was in exile. The etching was made by an art teacher called Emma Lowenstamm, a Czech Jew, who had brought the two men together. There is no proof of the work's authenticity, however.

The moves of the game were discovered later by chance. It was known that Hitler spent long evenings in Viennese cafés playing chess, especially after the art academy had twice rejected his application for admission. He was known as a fairly good player.

– He was a lousy military strategist, I said.

– *Gott sei Dank*, Igors said. Stalin also played chess, but not against Hitler.

– I wish all they had played was chess, I said.

– That's right, you have to follow the rules in chess.

Igors said he understood the instrumental value of chess. After the Second World War, the Soviet Union dominated international tournaments. Its top players were assisted by competent teams who helped them prepare for their games. Chess was seen as a mirror image of the Cold War, with its analysis of the adversary's strategy and its preparation of attacks to crush the opponent.

– How about your own game? I asked.

Igors started studying opening variations at a relatively late age, enabling him to improve his play even though he was old for a top player. Previously he had cared little about his status relative to his rivals, but improving his game increased his income. In the Soviet era, this had not been so important.

Igors thought chess was beautiful, like mathematics and music. The fascination of chess moves lies in the thoughts behind them, but also in the geometric compositions on the board. The aesthetic appeal of chess shields the ego from becoming inflated. If you cannot see the beauty of the game, it is hard to maintain your motivation. Although there is no shortage of time, prison walls hardly inspire inmates to play as obsessively as in fictional accounts.

I said that seeing the leaves of trees through the window opening in your cell may bring comfort and free the mind to travel. Someone once said he had escaped from prison without leaving his cell. It is said that the sight of trees from a hospital bed speeds up the patient's recovery. However, if you are serving a life sentence or permanently bedridden, a glimpse of the beauty of nature may depress you instead.

A friend of mine lived for decades while only being able to move one eyelid. This enabled him to express his thoughts, which remained lucid right to the end. Every summer the nurses offered to take him out into the open air, but he always refused.

I recalled that Marcel Duchamp once said that not all artists are chess players, but every good chess player is an artist. In contrast to art, he thought the creative element in chess has to be rationalized.

Duchamp was a fanatical chess player. Even on his honeymoon, he played and analysed chess positions from morning to night. I had read that his wife glued the pieces to the chessboard one night, but to no avail. They were divorced soon after the wedding. Duchamp's second wife was a keen chess player.

Igors said his life with Olita had been easy to the extent that they were both avid chess players. They even travelled to tournaments together, including the one in Jyväskylä.

Ajgul knew nothing about chess, but knew what to expect. Problems arose whenever Igors played too frequently and neglected her. Those problems were in the past now, but had been superseded by new ones.

– Shall we have a game now? Igors asked.

– Let's start, if you are willing, I quoted Pushkin's doomed duellist.

– Ten-minute games?

– Fine.

Igors put the chessboard on the table and set up the pieces. The table had a limp. I took my used boarding pass out of my pocket, folded it up and placed it under the table. There was no such trick to cure the limp in my game.

He hid a pawn in both hands and asked me to point at one. I got the white pieces and opened with the Queen's Gambit. Experience had shown that this should keep me out of trouble in the opening phase. This time, however, I lost a pawn without any positional compensation before we were even halfway through the game. In the games in the park, this would not have been decisive, but here it was.

In the next game, Igors played an opening variation I was not familiar with, and my position immediately became difficult. After a few quick moves, my defences crumbled. In the third game, I managed to avoid the position in the first game where I had lost a pawn and got into trouble. Towards the end, however, my position again collapsed, even though material was still equal.

That game reminded me of the final game I had lost on the ship. The end of that game had felt like waking with a start from a dream; I was in the middle of the Atlantic Ocean, with several days to go before reaching New York. This time, I was in a builders' shack in the middle of a grass-covered wasteland, hare territory. Spring frenzy could not have been further from my mind.

Igors tapped out a text message to his daughter, then set up the pieces again for a new game. This time I was on the brink of getting a draw, but was undone by time trouble. The first beep of the chess clock told me I had ten seconds left, and the second beep that I had lost on time. It is a horrible sound, except when the clock beeps for your opponent. In chess, too, time is merciless.

The opening of our last game followed well-trodden paths. Then Igors suddenly captured a pawn with his rook. For a moment, I thought he had made a decisive blunder, but this turned out to be wishful thinking. By sacrificing his rook, he obtained a decisive positional advantage. In the endgame, I knocked over my king to resign. Cunning sacrifices had been the hallmark of Mikhail Tal and many other masters.

Igors was just as deadly and efficient as I had expected. He made his moves quickly, made no mistakes, but confounded me with unexpected moves. Cancer or no cancer, his brain seemed to function with machine-like accuracy. FIDE may have deprived him of his grandmaster's title, but his playing strength had not been affected.

During the games, Igors made an approving comment whenever I found a good move. At the end, he said that Mikhail Tal, sitting on the edge of a cloud, had criticized some of my moves and had recommended better ones. Even in the hereafter, Tal could not keep his hands off the game.

Igors's face was expressionless when he played. There was nothing at stake in these games, but his posture must have stemmed from his time at the top. Chess professionals were either stone-faced or they faked reactions to confuse the opponent.

I thought that if he coached me, my level would skyrocket and I would become the star of the park. Afterwards, a brass memorial plaque would be nailed to the bench I always sat at, a feat that I would never achieve by any other means.

The day before, Igors had told me that every time he walked past Misha's monument, he thought of the games they had played. Misha never needed a matchstick during a game, for he would use the butt of his old cigarette to light a new one. Igors had lost most of their games; against Tal, even a draw was an achievement. Misha had said that he took his opponents into a deep, dark forest where two plus two is five and the path leading out is only wide enough for one.

He considered Tal an endearing personality who wanted everything from life. In fact, he was given a great deal, but always longed for something more. Perhaps he was a slave to his own genius. The last years of his life were overshadowed by illness, excessive drinking and morphine addiction. And yet he never accepted his own mortality.

In 1992, Tal was hospitalized. The attending physician racked his brain over ways to cheer up his illustrious patient. When he went to see Tal, he found the bed empty. No one knew where he had gone.

From the news, he learned that Tal had escaped from the hospital to take part in a blitz tournament in Moscow. There he beat Garry Kasparov, world champion at the time. That game was to be Tal's swan song.

Soon after, Tal died at the age of 55, according to Igors by his own hand. It was his way of resigning the game of life.

When Igors came back, I told him he had another text message waiting. I thanked him for the games and said I had received an excellent lesson. I understood why he did not want to play chess in the park.

Igors said that after Strasbourg he had played in a small blitz tournament in the Latvian city of Valka. This was possible because the tournament was not rated by FIDE. Nonetheless, he regretted having taken part. Today's games were the first he had played over the board since that tournament.

I started at the thought that if I had not drifted to Riga, he might never have played another game face to face with an opponent. I wondered what had been going on in his mind during our games, considering that he did not need to concentrate on them too hard.

– How did you feel about losing? I asked.

He said he had appreciated good moves and ingenious combinations even when his opponents had defeated him with them. Perhaps the other player had trained more diligently, or God had bestowed greater talent upon him. Therefore, why grieve at a loss?

For grandmaster Viktor Korchnoi, the most important, indeed the only object of the game was to crush his opponent. Igors thought that Korchnoi was the strongest grandmaster never to become world champion. Perhaps his obsession with victory was an obstacle to winning the championship.

Korchnoi continued to play at the top level long after he had turned seventy. He denied that he was clinging to past glory. Perhaps he wanted to show players who were half a century younger that they could still learn from him. In the Soviet Union, he was a hated defector, and the Soviet chess bureaucracy did everything in its power to prevent him from ever becoming world champion.

In pursuing victory, some players deliberately provoked their opponents. Igors told me about one grandmaster who blew cigarette smoke into his opponent's face. Maniacal stares, clicking one's finger joints and blowing bubbles of spit also worked.

Fischer was in the habit of correcting the position of his opponents' pieces if they were not dead centre on their squares. In a game played in Moscow, the burly Tigran Petrosian smashed his fist down on Fischer's fingers. That was the last time Fischer touched his opponent's pieces.

Igors had seen how Garry Kasparov always placed his watch on the table when the game started. When he believed he was gaining the upper hand, he put it back on his wrist. Since this habit was well-known, Kasparov used it to destabilize his opponent. He would also sometimes chuckle during the game for no obvious reason, or swear at a supposed mistake he had made. Sometimes the opponent would be tricked into making his next move quickly, making the exact mistake Kasparov was hoping for.

Most chess players are poor losers. Karl Marx was furious whenever he lost. Igors had witnessed adolescent tantrums by many a dignified player. On the other hand, winning is euphoric.

Once in a tournament in Odessa, grandmasters Tigran Petrosian and Viktor Korchnoi faced off for the umpteenth time. Igors knew them both as courteous gentlemen, but they were also fierce fighters. In that game, they kicked one another under the table, and the game had to be discontinued. They later expressed regret at their behaviour, which they explained was due to the extreme pressure they were under.

I told Igors about a German theatre director I once met in a village on the Spanish coast. He boasted about having won a tournament at a chess club in Paris. He considered himself a better player than me, although he lost most of our games. He thought he had had the advantage even in the games he lost. As reasons for losing he would cite time trouble, a serious blunder, loss of concentration or the dazzling sun, never his opponent's superiority. When I pointed out that he had made an illegal move, he lost his temper. Apparently it was not illegal in Paris.

When he won a game, he rewarded me with an arrogant look. His losses scratched his conceited ego, but gave me pleasure. I was particularly happy with a game that he lost on time. I had just one second left on my own clock.

I was nervous before the games, and my losses to him caused me physical discomfort, which surprised me. When discussing Rilke or Chekhov in a restaurant, he seemed another man entirely.

Perhaps this man of the theatre had played chess with his cast as the pieces. He probably reigned supreme in that game, perhaps also in the artistic sense. A leadership position in a large organization may make a person susceptible to behaving like this. Before my professional career went stale, I was a pawn on the bank's chessboard. This shielded me from arrogance, but caused other problems, for which I only had myself to blame since I had not heeded my heart's call.

On the same trip, I played chess against a Polish opponent. The mood was as different as night and day, and the games left me feeling euphoric. His wife told me that chess meant more to him than she and their children put together. I hope that was meant as a joke.

– It's true a person's attitude to chess mirrors their personality, Igors said.

– Yes, that goes for tennis as well, which I also played in Spain.

– A balanced person never blames his failures on other people, Igors said.

He told me a certain Jewish chess master interned in Auschwitz was forced to play chess with other prisoners as pieces. They stood on a giant chessboard. Whenever the master announced a move that captured one of the pieces, the prisoner representing that piece was summarily executed.

In the old days, chess masters wore a suit and tie. They were expected to say "check" whenever they threatened the opponent's king. If they threatened the queen, they said *garde*, meaning "look out for your queen". In those days, people played with their cards on the table, an attitude that Igors respected.

– That was also my grandfather's style, I said.

The star players one hundred years ago knew little opening theory, but they were geniuses in the middle game and focused on it. They played endgames with machine-like accuracy, as the top players still do. Modern masters were well-versed in opening theory, but Igors believed they would have had trouble playing against yesteryear's champions, who often diverged from orthodox play.

Someone knocked on the door. It was a worker bringing the keys. He shook hands with us and told Igors in Russian about an electrical problem that had lengthened his work day. He said he would carry on with the tiling of a bathroom tomorrow.

I said I was all thumbs in such work, and therefore had great respect for expert tilers. They were needed to guarantee future residents a good life. I assumed that the man did not speak Latvian. I had also noticed that almost all of the chess players in the park spoke Russian.

Igors observed that the man did indeed speak Latvian, but knew that Russian was Igors's mother tongue. As for the park crowd, there might be one or two among them who did not speak Latvian, which was why everyone spoke Russian. He had noticed the same phenomenon in Finland: if someone who did not speak Swedish happened to be among a group of Swedish-speaking Finns, everyone spoke Finnish.

Brecht discovered in Finland that my compatriots are silent in two languages. They did not experience this silence as awkward, however: they were adept at companionable silence and understood its value. To be sure, Finns can also be simply uncommunicative and rude, an attitude I had rarely encountered among Berliners.

I had not noticed any linguistic or political discord in the park, apart from some harmless teasing. I asked Igors how common such hostility was at the top level.

According to Igors, Kasparov was a hardheaded dissident and a befouler of his own nest who had no respect for his own country despite all the advantages it had afforded him. He had become the youngest world champion in chess history when he defeated his compatriot Anatoly Karpov in 1985.

Kasparov went on to defend his title successfully three times against Karpov, who was loyal to his country and the Communist Party. They were enemies, and their games represented a bitter political struggle. This was reflected in their expressions as they faced each other silently for days on end.

Later, when Kasparov was arrested at a demonstration, Karpov came to see him in prison, bringing a tasty meal with him. He swore it was not poisoned. Igors interpreted this visit as a gesture of respect and reconciliation.

I told him I had read that a self-proclaimed Kasparov fan once asked the champion to sign his chessboard. Having received the signature, he hit Kasparov on the head with the board and left, shouting that he loved Kasparov the chess master, but abhorred Kasparov the Putin critic.

Igors said such ambivalence was typical of Russia. Fischer was considered a chess genius, but as a human being he was – to put it nicely – a weirdo. The Fischer–Spassky match was the championship match of the century, but according to Igors treating it as a Cold War struggle was a Western media invention.

Fischer's victory was a personal one; it did not mean that the West had won, Igors said.

– But didn't it cause sorrow in the Soviet Union?

– Of course it led to criticism within the Soviet Chess Federation.

At a federation meeting, Mikhail Botvinnik said Spassky had lost because he treated Fischer as a friend. If you want to win the world championship, you have to treat your opponent as a personal enemy. Fischer – like Kasparov – sought to crush his opponent's ego. Igors could not understand such a vitriolic attitude.

Botvinnik himself had shared first place with Capablanca, who was Cuban, at a tournament in Nottingham back in 1936. After the tournament, *Pravda* published a letter from Botvinnik to Stalin attributing his victory to the beloved leader. Igors told me that someone had called Botvinnik from Moscow to inform him that he had written and posted such a letter.

The class struggle was illustrated in various parts of the Soviet Union with chess tours during which the two sides were represented by Red Army soldiers dressed in white and black cloaks. The white side represented workers and the black side capital. It is not hard to guess which side always won. According to Igors, this was Socialist Realism at its most basic.

A Peruvian friend of mine who lived in Berlin had a chess set in which the white pieces were Incas and the black pieces were Spanish conquistadors. The Spaniards had an enormous superiority in arms, but on the chessboard the two sides were evenly matched. The Inca warriors bore the *chakana*, the Inca cross, on their shields. The three steps on the cross symbolised the upper world, this world and the underworld. The knights were replaced by llamas. The pieces were so ornate that it was hard to play with them. Moreover, winning with the black pieces made you feel like a real conquistador. On the other hand, you did not want to throw the game either.

– What's the purpose of chess in your view? I asked.

– The game in itself has no purpose. It is just a curious game in which wooden pieces are moved back and forth according to a set of strange rules.

Of course, as a coach, Igors could not actually say this to the children and young people he coached. The important thing was that they should grow up to be decent people who got on in life. Some people devote their lives to collecting stamps, others to growing rare tulip varieties. There are many paths to the kingdom of heaven.

Chess builds character. It is a gym for the mind, and studying chess teaches teamwork. Thus, for Igors, coaching had become more important than playing. Unlike in the game itself, one could not make serious blunders as a coach. Moreover, he earned more from coaching, which had become increasingly important to him in recent years.

Meanwhile, as the pressure on him as a player had intensified, the joy of playing had diminished. Playing chess without joy was a sheer waste of time.

Igors thought there was no point for a mentally alert person to get stuck in the monastic miniature world of chess. It was a road to nowhere. He had regularly reminded himself of this during his career.

Emanuel Lasker, the longest-reigning world champion, once met a promising young player who dreamed of becoming a grandmaster. Lasker warned him to avoid dedicating himself to chess. There were more important things in life. At the time, the young man was shocked by this advice, but he was grateful later.

Ajgul called to remind Igors to collect his medicine from the pharmacy. Igors said he would go in the morning and wished his wife good night.

I picked up a bishop and twiddled it between my fingers.

– That tournament in Strasbourg, I said and glanced at him inquiringly.

Igors glanced out at the fading evening and leaned back in his chair. It had happened on a radiant July day. The Strasbourg Open was being played in the dreamily beautiful Parc de l'Orangerie. He sighed.

– I should never have played there.

– Why not?

He had been taking strong cancer medication before the tournament and was unwell, but needed the prize money to pay for his expensive treatment. Moreover, his tournament successes had always meant better pay for team matches. He admitted that ambition was also a factor; a good foot soldier dreaming of becoming a general.

Igors knew that he was under suspicion. He asked the Algerian chief arbiter whether he could leave his mobile phone on the arbiter's desk. The arbiter replied that this was possible, but he could not guarantee that the phone would still be there at the end of the tournament. He thought it would be safer for Igors to keep it in his pocket.

In the decisive game, he faced Roman Skomorokhin, a Russian player who was younger than Igors and ranked a good deal lower. Igors was the only grandmaster taking part, and he should have won routinely. They shook hands, praised the venue and exchanged pleasantries.

Igors said he could only see the board hazily. He was reminded of the aged opponent he had played in Sevastopol over forty years earlier. The old man had had to resign because of exhaustion. Now he was in the old man's position, and feared the same fate.

In the middlegame, Igors was uncertain which player had the advantage. Because of his illness, he had to visit the invalid toilet frequently. He thought he could use his mobile phone without any problems there, and took it out on an impulse. He set up the position on a chess app, which stated that his position was so strong he could not possibly lose. He did not even look at the move proposed by the app.

When he returned to the board, a crowd of people had gathered around the chief arbiter's desk. He was shown a photo taken of him looking at his phone screen in the toilet. He immediately confessed to using the app, tipped over his king, shook his opponent's hand, signed a written confession and left the tournament.

The birds in the park sang as if nothing had happened. He found a bench on which he could sit with his back to the pavilion. Gradually his hazy vision brightened. He could make out the sea of flowers, and he breathed in their scent avidly.

A ladybird landed on the back of his hand. It stood still for a moment, as if wondering where on earth it had landed. Then it crawled slowly along a vein, turned back and stopped again. It too seemed confused.

Cities and tournaments he had played in hovered at the back of his mind like mirages. He also felt a flicker of the ecstasy arising from winning a particularly good game. In his mind, he replayed the critical moves in the game that won him the Latvian championship in 1995. Then the imaginary chessboard and pieces dissolved among the blossoms.

He knew there would be no return. His foremost thought was relief.

The photo did not show what was on his screen. Igors said the chess grid had been photoshopped as further evidence against him. FIDE published the fake image on its website and banned him from competition for six years. The photo was disseminated in social media posts around the world, and it was also published in US mainstream publications. The name of the photographer was never revealed.

When he returned from Strasbourg to Riga, there were other chess players on the same flight. There was hatred in their eyes. When he got home, he told everyone what had happened, including at school. Some of his pupils left, but most of them continued under his coaching.

Some friends turned their back on him, which Igors said he could understand. A few top players who knew he was in financial straits offered to help, but he refused. One of his former pupils, Alexei Shirov, transferred money to his account without telling him. In his prime, Shirov had been ranked No. 2 in the world.

I told Igors I had seen a post on the internet in which Shirov said Rausis was a fantastic coach and mentor. Igors said they had first worked together during the Soviet period, and he had good memories of those days.

After Strasbourg, Igors considered giving up chess completely. He had acted wrongly and accepted the long ban without complaint. He was prepared to carry his cross all the way to the site of his execution.

It was a crime to install a camera in the toilet, as it was to take and publish the photograph. A couple of lawyers contacted him and urged him to defend his rights. They even promised to bring charges against the organizers and FIDE *pro bono*, but he was not interested. What was done could not be undone, and a legal process would not have changed anything.

I said if I had not seen that photo on the internet, I would not be sitting there now. An ordinary news item hardly would have disturbed me for long. I could not understand the candid camera or the way FIDE had proceeded. To be sure, I had also wondered about his reasons for cheating, and the consequences.

The interview published in conjunction with the photo had made me think about the sacrifices required to reach the top and to stay there, and about the relationship between chess and life in general. These musings were marked by our shared experience of terminal illness.

I also said I had thought about situations in which I myself had cheated. However, I did not tell Igors about the ruse I had resorted to in order to find his shack.

Igors admitted that he had used a chess program twice before. After a game against the No. 1 player of the Czech Republic, his opponent could not believe that Igors had come up with a certain brilliant move without the help of a computer. He wrote about his suspicions in an article, saying that the belated increase in Rausis's playing strength could not have been possible with any 'clean' method.

According to Igors, the player in question had no grounds for his suspicions. He either did not know or ignored the fact that Igors had already been among the world's top 50 players back in the early 1990s. In those days, computer programs of the modern kind were not even available yet.

Igors later played against the same opponent on two occasions. He said he used a computer twice in those games. He was provoked by the accusations and acted in revenge. This did not help, however, since he lost both games.

He showed me his battered iPhone, which could be used by any amateur to defeat Magnus Carlsen, the world champion. Carlsen's rating was around 2 860 at the time, while the rating of the free Stockfish program was 3 600. In a game between the two, Carlsen would have had a two per cent chance of getting a draw.

According to Igors, the computer chess app, a creation of the untiring human mind, was an invitation to cheat. The internet community chess.com had had to close tens of thousands of accounts because of cheating. Using mobile phones was forbidden in major tournaments, but electronic chips that were easy to conceal were being developed to facilitate communication with the outside world during games.

Igors claimed that he had played against many cheaters, but this did not excuse his transgression. There was rarely any cheating in team tournaments: a misdeed by just one player would cause the whole team to be charged.

I mentioned that I had read that world champion Garry Kasparov had accused the IBM team behind the Deep Blue supercomputer of cheating.

– What was all that about? I asked.

Deep Blue beat Kasparov for the first time in 1997. Igors said the program calculated 200 million possible moves per second, evaluated the resulting position and selected the best option. There was plenty to calculate, since just the first four moves can be played in tens of billions of different ways, and there are more possible variations of chess games than there are atoms in the observable universe.

In their 1997 match, Kasparov and Deep Blue played six games. Kasparov won the first. In the second game, the computer played an unexpected move that surprised Kasparov so much that he resigned. The next three games were drawn. In the last game, the computer sacrificed a knight, with the result that Kasparov's position collapsed.

Kasparov asserted that the computer's creative winning moves should not have been possible considering its state of development at the time, and that IBM had cheated by hiring strong players to assist it. Igors thought Kasparov's accusation credible. Losing again would have damaged IBM's reputation. As it was, the company's stock price rose significantly following the match.

I remembered *Newsweek* describing the world champion's loss as the desperate last stand of the human brain. The result was compared with the Apollo moon landing. I did not think that was one of mankind's star moments either. There was plenty of more urgent business back on Earth.

According to Igors, the computer did not imitate human creativity and intuition, but played like a machine. Its victory was not due to intelligence, but to its prodigious powers of calculation. Kasparov wrote: "Deep Blue was intelligent the way your programmable alarm clock is intelligent. Not that losing to a $10 million alarm clock made me feel any better." He admitted to being a poor loser.

Igors thought the evolution of computer chess had eroded the magic of chess. The people who created the chess-playing computer destroyed the character of the game, replacing adventurous variations and sacrifices with mechanically calculated sequences of moves. Players could no longer trust one another.

Magnus Carlsen was also opposed to computer chess. He relied on his strong intuition, which enabled him to confuse his opponent by making moves the computer would not have recommended.

Igors said cheating was not a recent invention. When the two best Soviet women played in the final of a chess tournament, the coach of one stood next to the board and tried to signal the winning move to his protégée. He kept his thumbs in his pocket and showed the move in an eight-finger code agreed in advance. For some reason or another, the advice did not register. The clock ticked. The coach went to a nearby bar, where men were imbibing a popular drink, half beer and half vodka.

– Who would like to earn five rubles? the coach asked.

– What do I have to do for it? the man sitting next to him asked.

– Go to the hall on the second floor in the building next door and shout: bishop to g3!

– What does it mean?

– Never mind, just do it!

The man did as he was told. Officials tried to grab him, but he managed to get past them. Igors said the coach's protégée had won thanks to that move. Five rubles gave the messenger the chance to booze up all evening on a more expensive tipple, a mix of brandy and champagne.

Igors felt that the concept of cheating was ambiguous. In a game between the Ukrainian grandmasters and friends Ruslan Ponomariov and Vasyl Ivanchuk, Ponomariov found himself in a difficult position and was about to resign. He looked out the window and saw a decrepit car with no wheels. He asked Ivanchuk whether he could see the car too and wondered whose car it was. Vasyl replied: "Nichya!" In a flash, Ruslan stretched out his hand and said he agreed. Taken aback, Vasyl gripped the offered hand. The word means both 'draw' and 'no one's'. Thus Ponomariov avoided certain defeat.

In any case, the chess path was closed for now as far as Igors was concerned, but thanks to the events in Strasbourg he was still alive. Until then, he had refused radiotherapy, which would have made it impossible for him to play. After Strasbourg, he began to look after his health, agreed to the treatments proposed and also allowed Ajgul to take care of him. His doctors applauded these changes.

He said he felt better now than before and during the tournament. Maybe he had half-consciously hoped to be caught; it was a kind of sporting suicide.

Perhaps God had shown him a path to salvation by abandoning competitive chess. It would have been foolish not to seize the opportunity.

Be that as it may, what he had done was wrong. It was a kind of theft. He had admitted as much to everyone, whatever the reasons for his act had been. He wished to emphasize this particularly for the sake of his pupils, which was also why he had agreed to an interview.

He would simply have to live with the shame. He still saw ill will in the eyes of other chess players, although some of his colleagues had sided with him. People he did not know had also expressed support.

He was particularly sorry on behalf of his family. He had even changed his name to protect them. Rausis was a contaminated name, so he dropped it. For the second time, he adopted his wife's surname, and now went by the name of Isa Kasimi.

I thanked him for the evening and the games and told him he would remain Igors to me. At the gate, I asked him one last question: if he were a young man fresh out of school, would he do something differently? He replied that he would make the same choices and even repeat the Strasbourg episode. However, he would try to treat his wives more gently.

– Shall we meet again tomorrow evening? Igors asked.

– Gladly. It's my last night in Riga.

– Let's text about the time.

We embraced for goodbye. Igors set off on his rounds, disappearing behind the neighbouring building. Of all the night-watchmen in the world, he must have been the most proficient in foreign languages and chess. He had no use for these skills in his job, however, and they were not reflected on his pay slip.

After his rounds, he would sit down at the table, turn on the radio and take out his thermos flask and the salami sandwiches made by Ajgul. The hours would crawl by: another night without incident. Then the new day would dawn, and the world would come alive again. His shift would last a few more hours, after which he would pack his few possessions, take his stick off the hook and hobble back to downtown Riga. He would repeat this routine day after day and night after night, until the houses were completed and the shack was moved to another site.

According to some guru or another, our sorrows are due to our inability to stay in one place. He called on those besotted with the quest for happiness to settle for the devotion of a monastic cell. Perhaps Igors thought so too, now that he had nothing else left.

Dostoevsky was also in the habit of working in a shack all through the night, sipping cold tea. He realized one night that he was a child of God, and felt a joy without which existence is meaningless. Igors probably found joy by reliving his early moments of happiness.

I had imagined that he would regret his cheating, but mostly he was sorry only because of his family. Since he could not undo what was done, perhaps he preferred to think it had all been for the best. Gustav also said he regretted nothing, but the way he said it was more convincing.

I thought about moments and situations I would like to relive in order to do things differently. I was immediately reminded of childhood springs by the seaside. I would take off my shirt only for a short time to avoid singeing the skin of my upper body. It had proved to have a long memory.

The air had cooled, and mist swirled above the grass, whiffs of a dreamworld. Dense clumps of nettle grew next to the fence like those I had seen a goat eat in Russian East Karelia. The farmer told me he crushed goats' bones for chicken feed with a Heureka bone grinder that he had received as a gift from Finland. There was probably nothing strange for him about people dying. Unlike humans, however, goats were blissfully unaware that they would die one day.

My sheep did not care for nettles, but they were wild about dried bread crusts. When I first acquired them as lambs from a breeder, I made the mistake of assuming that sheep were simple animals. The farmer took offence, saying that sheep were consummate artists of their own life, unlike human beings, who fill their heads with trivialities and then go on to mess up both their own lives and the whole world. According to the sheep farmer, if God had created man in his image, the result did neither of them any credit.

I texted Igors from the hotel breakfast room to ask him what he was doing during the day. There was no answer; perhaps he was still asleep.

I had a second cup of coffee and spread strawberry marmalade over my croissant. The women at the table next to mine were speaking Finnish. They had taken the ferry to Tallinn and driven from there to Riga. I listened to how they were going to prepare their pets for the day's dog show, but held my tongue. This was not a subject I wished to discuss. Cat shows were pure cruelty to animals; cats had to sit in glass boxes with nowhere to hide from sight.

Whenever a Finnish friend of mine heard someone speak our language in the streets of Prague, he said to me in a loud voice: "Komm schon, Heinrich". This friend had worked for the UN in the past. He was accompanying Finland's Prime Minister Harri Holkeri to a meeting when a beautiful, exotic-looking woman entered the lift they were in. Holkeri said to my friend in Finnish that she would make a good lay. The lady did not bat an eyelid. As all three got off, she said "Have a nice day" in Finnish.

I turned on my iPad and watched the game between Hitler and Lenin to which Igors had sent me a link. Adolf opened energetically, making sensible moves, but then made a couple of mistakes which turned the game inexorably in Vladimir's favour.

In a hopeless position, Adolf had the good sense to resign before Vladimir could deliver the *coup de grâce*. On the basis of this game, I felt that I could have beaten Adolf, but would have had a hard time with Vladimir.

I re-sent my text message. No reply. Normally Igors had reacted swiftly to my texts. I reckoned that something untoward must have happened. Whatever it was, Ajgul would know about it, and I hoped to find her at home.

I polished off my croissant and set off to look for the house on the edge of Vērmanes Park where Ajgul and Igors lived. Fortunately I had written down the address. I bought a bunch of tulips to be on the safe side.

The magnificent lobby, with paintings and crystal chandeliers, gave me pause. It was like entering a church. This lobby must have stunned and humbled the bank's customers. To be sure, I did not know whether people had come begging for a loan, hat in hand, in those days.

I was briefly reminded of the Bank of Finland's stately staircase decorated with a stained-glass triptych by Juho Rissanen. This work, familiar to me after working in the building for a quarter of a century, depicted a rural Finland of which only fragments remained and for which I frequently felt nostalgic.

My efforts to steer the Finnish economy in the kind of sustainable direction depicted by Rissanen had been delusional. That house rejected the role of a utopian haven; banks were banks, that was a truth you simply had to accept. Once I had grasped this, I resigned myself to simply earning my daily bread.

The flat was on the first floor. I entered the lift, a museum piece, and sat down on the curved mahogany bench. Taking the lift just to go one flight up seemed silly, but the call of its beauty was irresistible. The lift gave a jerk and slowly creaked upward. The mirror showed the image of a man with a concerned expression, but this had nothing to do with the lift.

Ajgul opened the plain door, invited me in, held out a pair of carpet slippers and shook my hand.

– Igors had warm words for your moments together, she said in German.

– They were memorable, I said.

– It's nice to meet you in person.

– The pleasure is all mine, I said and handed her the tulips.

Ajgul said Igors had fainted in the morning. He had been rushed to hospital in an ambulance. Ajgul had gone with him, but had been refused entry to the hospital due to covid rules. This was not the first time. Igors had had to remain in hospital under observation. His condition did not appear to give cause for alarm.

I sat down at the table. Ajgul took a crystal vase out of a cupboard, filled it with water and arranged the tulips in it. She was a slight woman with an air of dignity and warmth. She spoke melodious German and looked me in the eye when she spoke. I could sense her literary erudition, even though we had not yet spoken a word about books.

The vase reflected the sun's rays, casting a rainbow arc on the wall. The room was about five metres high, with a loft bed built of wood. There was a kitchenette with a movable hob. The flat and its furnishings were ascetic, and less spacious than my bedroom in Berlin.

I recognised the large eyes and noses of two puppets on the window sill: Spejbl and Hurvinek, Czech cult figures from half a century ago. I knew they dated from the same period as East Germany's Little Sandman, that gentle ambassador of a dictatorship.

– Would you like tea or coffee? Ajgul asked.

– Coffee, *bitte*. Do you mind if we call each other *Du*?

– I find it a little awkward to say *Du* to an older man.

– *Wie Sie wollen*, as you please.

Ajgul knew that Igors and I had agreed to meet later that evening. Igors had promised to get in touch when he knew more about his situation.

– Igors had charming words for you, I said. How did you get to know each other?

She laughed and blushed faintly. They had been sitting face to face on a minibus going to Paris, but had not talked, as they did not expect to have a common language. When they showed their passports on the French border, it turned out that they had the same mother tongue, Russian. She was a tourist; Igors was going to a chess tournament.

When they arrived, they walked together towards their hotels, which were close to one another. In the street, they ran into a young man who stopped to chat with Igors. When he left, Igors said that was Viswanathan Anand from India, also known as the Tiger of Madras after his birthplace, and world junior chess champion at the time. Anand came from a religious family and was a believer himself. He later became world champion.

Ajgul said she did not play chess and did not know any chess players, but she thought the game sublime and was impressed by the meeting between Igors and Anand, who were both charming gentlemen.

Igors suggested meeting at some café the next evening. They exchanged hotel addresses. Ajgul had some doubts, as she had realized that Igors was married. Nonetheless, she agreed to meet him.

The upshot was that at the end of the week they travelled together from Paris to Bonn, where Ajgul was living and teaching classical German literature. At this point, Igors was unemployed, but that did not worry him. This had happened about thirty years ago.

Their days in Paris and Bonn had been a happy time for Ajgul, but the events in Strasbourg two years ago had come as a shock. Not only had Igors let himself down; he had dragged his family into the dirt with him. The attitude of people Igors did not even know had also been affected.

Ajgul served me a slice of an apple tart that she had baked and brought a jug of cream to the table. She sighed and said she had tried to understand his deceit and to forgive him, but had succeeded only in part.

It became clear that Strasbourg had not been the first time he had cheated. Ajgul assumed that there had been more incidents than Igors had admitted to. She considered her husband a gambler who was unable to stop cheating even when the rumours started flying. He was like Dostoevsky, who would not leave the casino until he had lost his last ruble.

Ajgul said she identified with Anna Dostoevskaya, who had suffered from her husband's gambling addiction. Once when Fyodor had lost all their money once again, he had kneeled before Anna, sobbing, and implored his wife to forgive him. Igors was not a man of such theatrical gestures, nor would Ajgul have wanted them.

I told her about an acquaintance of mine who entered a casino for the first time in his life after an evening's drinking. He bet all his money on a single number, and the ball stopped at that number. He won four thousand euros. In the morning he had a pang of conscience, considering his winnings undeserved. He donated the whole sum to a children's cancer foundation.

No such luck for Igors. Ajgul said the misstep had ruined his chess career; gone were his joy in playing, the trips to tournaments and the colleagues who had been important to him. All these had been replaced by shame. After a cosmopolitan career, he had become a refugee in his own country.

Ajgul said that Igors had only gradually realized what he had lost. A total collapse is often needed before one understands the value of one's previous life. Fortunately he had not followed the example of many chess masters by descending into insanity. However, Ajgul did not understand her husband's notion that the incident was a message sent by God and had saved his life. For her, he was merely trying to hide behind God's back. Perhaps he had read Tolstoy, who encouraged human beings to seek salvation with the energy provided by their errors.

Igors claimed that he had played against many cheaters over the years, by which he tried to relativize his misdeed. Ajgul considered this a feeble defence, as was his emphasis on his need for the prize money. Once he had betrayed his principles, there was little chance that he could maintain a healthy attitude to life. He would have to grapple with his failure as long as he lived.

Although his act had made Igors neglect Ajgul, she could not shirk her responsibility for him on account of his illness. Neither could she judge him nor erase him from her life. Nonetheless, his dishonesty had created a distance between them.

– We are two different people, and I just have to accept it, she said.

– Some people never understand that, I said.

Igors had told me that chess had been his gateway to the world. I said that his stories had opened up for me a perspective on grandmaster chess, a world that seemed fascinating but also merciless. I admired the way he faced his illness and the approaching end. I had expected to find a sad man seeking to evade the sore spots in his life.

– Igors has made a virtue of necessity, Ajgul said.

Despite this, Ajgul would have preferred to have him understand and accept the inevitable effects of ageing and illness in time instead of cloistering himself in his game world. People do not know themselves, and sometimes act in ways that no one else can understand or that even they themselves cannot understand. External incitements may provoke incomprehensible actions.

– Everyone should understand that life means resignation, Ajgul said.

– That's something I'm trying to learn…

She said she would like to go back to her university in Bonn. She still had friends there who had promised to help. If it worked out, Igors would have to come with her. For once, she said with a brief smile, then added that Igors had nothing against moving to Germany. There no one would be likely to know him or be aware of the mortifying end to his chess career.

I said that if they ever had business in Berlin, it would be a pleasure and an honour to host them there. My guestroom was usually vacant. I gave Ajgul my phone number and e-mail address and asked her to get in touch if something happened to Igors to make him unable to contact me.

As I was leaving, Ajgul wrapped up another slice of apple tart for me. She said that Igors hoped I would visit Riga again.

– Inshallah, I said.

I put my shoes back on, gave Ajgul a hug and pressed the opal lift button. The mirror reflected the same male face, but the lines in his forehead were gone.

It struck me that not only did Ajgul and Anna Dostoevskaya share a common fate; they were also kindred spirits. I can visualize them sitting by a samovar, discussing Dostoevsky's novella *The Gambler*. They are drinking tea, gazing through an open window towards an orchard in which the cherry blossoms have just opened, turning the world into a place of dreamlike beauty.

In the evening, I wandered the city streets in a new direction. In one of the more remote neighbourhoods of Riga, small businesses had dressed their windows with cutesy folk art. Advertising slogans were traced on cardboard in coloured ink. In one sign, the letters tapered off towards the edge to make the text fit. A porcelain pig in the window of a butcher's shop could have been the half-brother of my piggy bank.

The compositions reproduced the shop windows of the Helsinki of my childhood. In the eyes of the little boy that I still was, the shops of that period had always existed; what had come afterwards was new.

The window of a photographer's studio displayed a child stroking a dog, an old man with a peaceful aura, and a married couple kissing. That is how we wish to see life, and studio photographers give us our wish. In Igors's Sevastopol, such images had represented the official truth about life, and the people who produced them had been creatures of the state machine.

The window of a shoe shop displayed women's slippers with a pink bobble at the toe, a dash of superfluous beauty. My shoes should last for the rest of my journey. No more need to visit shoe shops. As for shirts, hats and scarves, I had enough to last several lifetimes.

I stared at my reflection in the window. Was that geriatric grey-beard really me? I looked like a prisoner of war at the edge of a sandpit who has just refused his last cigarette. The comparison was not far removed from reality.

When I was a child, I was told that if I stared into a mirror too long, I would see a monkey. Half a century ago, I became aware of the clean-shaven face reflected in the window of my office at the central bank. It was summer, but I was not yet entitled to a holiday, which alerted me to the harsh reality. Here I will sit for the next four decades, and can do no other, I thought.

On an Interrail trip, I spent a night at the run-down Grand Hotel in Wrocław. The gilt floral frame of the mirror in my room reflected a man halfway through his working career. The crumbling mercury surface of the mirror gave the image a superficial and ephemeral aspect, as if I was looking at myself with someone else's eyes. I had wished for a magic mirror to show what I had locked up inside.

I knew the Grand Hotel would revert to its former glory, whereas I myself would decay. I was not worried about wrinkles and creases, but I hoped that they would not turn into furrows of bitterness.

Once I dreamed that I arrived at the edge of a lake in the wilds. I bent down to gaze at its smooth surface. I could not see my reflection. I did not exist.

A light went on in the shoe shop, obscuring my reflection. The turning points in my life passed before my eyes as in a film on fast forward. Between them had passed whole years of which I had only fragmentary memories. Reading my old letters and diaries, I had noticed that time could distort my memories, embellishing and altering them. I had also made moves that should never have been made. What would be my last move?

A white feather wafted through the air, landing at my feet. I glanced up, but there was no bird in sight, nor anyone dusting off bedclothes on a balcony. I picked up the feather and put it in my pocket as a souvenir. At that moment, my phone beeped. Igors wrote to say he would have to stay in hospital for observation. His room was comfortable; he was receiving good care and eating good food. Don't worry about me, all is well, he wrote.

I was a little doubtful about his reassurances. Any message could be his last. A bright outlook on life cannot sustain you forever. Fruitless thoughts, but I thought them anyway.

I would return to Berlin one experience the richer. So what? I would continue to play and study the theory of chess obsessively. What was the point? Beating Daniel would not change anything either. My plight would remain desperate until it was time for my last supper. No amount of cheating, prayer or pills could save my puny life.

If someone were to write my obituary, I would never see it, and even if I did, I would hardly be able to read it without blushing. Perhaps I should write it myself. If it was honest, it would not be published.

What if Ajgul should ask me to write Igors's obituary? A long, distinguished career as a chess player and coach in various parts of the world, acquainted with chess legends, teacher of hundreds of children in Riga, known as a considerate and warm-hearted man. And yet the chess world would only remember his cheating, which could not be passed over. I would have to slip in a sentence that aroused sympathy and understanding for his lapse.

To judge by obituaries, the world was peopled by kind-hearted, responsible men and women with a wonderful sense of humour who radiated joy and neighbourly love towards everyone around them. What a pity they were never told during their lifetime what paragons they would become once they were dead. Conflict, disorder, resentment, spite and imperfection would remain the blight of the living.

Once I saw a funeral wreath with a card bearing the text: "You managed to stay nasty to the end." A hare had chewed the carnations in the wreath. At the cemetery, a man asked if he was allowed to jump up and down on his mother-in-law's grave. Caught off guard, the caretaker could not think of any rule or regulation that forbade it. A Finnish writer wrote that he had stubbed out his cigarette on his father's grave.

In the *Spoon River Anthology* by Edgar Lee Masters, the inhabitants of an American town recount their lives from the grave. In one story, a character called Hoheimer, having stolen pigs from a local farmer, runs away to join the army and ends up with a bullet in his heart. Lying under a marble statue, he wonders what the words *Pro Patria*, carved in the granite pedestal, even mean.

Some obituaries said that their subject had died prematurely. The intended meaning was perhaps "unexpectedly or unnaturally young, without being struck by a fatal illness". The writers may have been thinking of an appropriate lifespan as the benchmark. Mercifully, no one knows when their hour will come.

I let my feet take me where they would, drifting through a landscape that was as close to a dream as reality could ever be. Dusk was falling, and the street ahead merged into the distant haze. Above it all, a cloud formation towered like a snow-clad mountain, inviting me to climb it. From the top, Riga's street network, parks, branching rivers, church yards and harbours would spread out beneath my feet. The living and the dead have testified to the beauty and joy of life, to its atrocities and savagery. The hurly-burly continues, without ever producing anything enduring.

I was aroused from my reverie when a fox slipped out of the park and ran across the street, stopping in front of me. It froze for a moment, staring at me as if it was trying to impart a message. I wondered which of us was in the wrong place. Then it trotted off into the shadows in the park. It was living in the moment like a child, never stopping to regret its missteps, if indeed that is what they could be called.

I stopped and leaned on a lamp post. Moths were fluttering about the light source, and a bat swept past. Bats were considered messengers of evil. In Spain they were thought to bring luck. Whom to believe?

In the cone of light, I saw myself as the wandering film star in some Italian Neo-Realist film, although I could not remember which one. All that was missing was the cigarette dangling from his jaw.

In my bag I had the case of hand-rolled cigarettes that I had picked up on the train to Jurmala. If this was not the moment to smoke the first cigarette in my life, when then? I bummed a light from a passer-by, lit a fag and blew smoke rings into the cooling air. They turned into gauze and vanished out of sight.

The flashing neon sign of a pizzeria alerted me to the fact that I had not eaten anything since Ajgul's apple tart. There were some inviting-looking restaurants in this part of town.

I wound up at a café with assorted furniture and large paintings of the street art kind on the walls. The bar counter was built of rough-sawn planks, and above it hung a rusty metal plaque bearing the English text "In Marx and Engels We Trust – All Others Pay Cash". A ventilation duct made of sheet metal ran across the ceiling. The clientele displayed the same casual style: birds of a feather flocked together, as they did at my regular haunt, the Al Hamra. Here too, many of the clients seemed to know one another. I could not imagine Igors coming here.

The speakers were playing Nick Cave. *Death Is Not the End* gave me a thrill. What did Cave think you could expect after death? Milk and honey and harp music perhaps?

I now envied those to whom faith in life after death brought succour and who looked to the clouds for signs of a better life. On the other hand, this seemed like a naive attempt to escape. When a little girl I knew died of leukaemia, her mother said a loving angel had come to take her to the kingdom of heaven.

If I had spent more time in Ajgul's company, I would have asked her about death and the hereafter, which had been the subject of her doctoral thesis. For Muslims, death is a community matter, but Ajgul probably had no other members of her tribe living in Riga. Her faith seemed pure, without the hint of instrumentality in Igors's religion.

It also occurred to me that I could have invited Ajgul to dinner on my last night in Riga, but that might have seemed odd, given that Igors was in hospital. On the other hand, I had no idea whether she would have had the time or inclination to accept. I would not have a second opportunity.

I hoped that Ajgul would return to Bonn to teach at the university. She said she had enjoyed the work, and it would give her security for the rest of her life, since Igors was likely to depart first. In the fishing villages of Brittany, candles would be lit during a wedding ceremony, and the candle that went out first showed which of the newlyweds would pass away first. Why did they need to know? I did not dare ask Ajgul why she had agreed to leave Bonn in the first place. Although she had a mind of her own, she was no standard-bearer of feminism.

I sat down in a rattan chair at a table by the window and examined the menu. Nowadays one could be confident that the items printed on the menu existed. In the Soviet period, they tended to show what the restaurant had run out of.

In Tallinn, I had once ordered chocolate ice cream with whipped cream for dessert. The restaurant had run out of ice cream, but the waiter brought me a double serving of whipped cream to make up for it. On average, the fried chicken was prepared to perfection: burnt on the outside and frozen on the inside. The chef had been sent the recipe from Moscow.

On that same trip, I had had the idea of photographing a chicken farm, a *sovkhoz* collective with more birds than there were people in Estonia. I introduced myself at the gate as a reporter for the Finnish magazine *Siipikarja* (Poultry). The director of the *sovkhoz* came to meet me. He said he always read the magazine in question from cover to cover. Fortunately he did not say anything more about it.

The director offered me cabbage pasties in the canteen, strewing them with chives. After lunch, I was given a white lab coat and boots to put on. As we strolled among the sea of cages, he told me about the collective's production target, which it had exceeded once again. It occurred to me that they had bred the shock workers of the chicken world.

I ordered a chèvre salad and a glass of Georgian red wine. The waiter said in English that she knew the wine grower, who sent her batches of wine direct. For young people like her, learning Russian was no longer compulsory. Many of them seemed to associate the language with past Soviet rule, which few Latvian-speakers appreciated.

A woman flitted past between the tables, pausing to speak to a few customers. To judge by their expressions, what she said was amusing. I felt sure that her good humour was not something imposed on her by her boss. Perhaps she was the boss. I wondered whether she voted for the Left or the Greens, not that it made any difference.

As I waited for my salad, I leafed through my travel reading, a volume of poetry called *Heart on the Pavement* by the Latvian poet Aleksandrs Čaks.

Čaks described the seamy side of his beloved Riga: old women selling newspapers, guttersnipes, whores, coal men. In one of his poems, a workman tosses a musician a two-lati coin, telling him to play Chopin's *Marche funèbre*. The musician jumps up in anger: a funeral march in a tavern, what impudence!

Like Pushkin and other classic Russian authors, Čaks seems to have thought commoners genuine. Powerful people were more likely to be crooks; it was said that no palace was ever built with virtuous acts.

The introduction to the volume points out that Čaks's poetry was branded as anti-Soviet in its time, and his works were banned. In later years his poetry became more obeisant. As the Finns say, Siberia teaches you.

The book quotes the Latvian-born poet Astrīde Ivaska, according to whom both weeping and singing are a part of life and we should be thankful for that. A moving sentiment, although I do not know whom she thought we should thank. Igors might have said something similar, though not as poetically.

I had not glimpsed Čaks's seamy side of Riga. Perhaps it was already lost. The goings-on described by Čaks had also characterized Helsinki's Punavuori district in my childhood, until it was hit by the demolition craze and turned into a trendy neighbourhood. The proletarian decades of Berlin's Prenzlauer Berg were also just a dim memory.

At the table next to mine, a young man was playing chess on a laptop. He seemed to be using his mobile phone to consult a chess program. Two chess apps were taking each other's measure, so the player could not be accused of cheating.

I put my book aside and thought about Igors's style of play during his competitive years. He said he had his strong buttocks to thank for his success, and described his style as boring. Perhaps this had to do with his illness, but there was a touch of modesty involved too. Shirov thought many of Igors's games were inspired.

The Cuban world champion Capablanca suffered from high blood pressure, for which there was virtually no treatment a century ago. The excitement of the game raised it even further, and led him to make mistakes. He tried to play simply and calmly, but died of a cerebral haemorrhage at the age of 53.

Since a game can last seven hours, it is tough even for physically fit players. Fischer once said that a player's strength reflects his physical fitness; body and mind cannot be separated. Karpov said he had lost ten kilos during his matches against Kasparov.

Anyone familiar with the key games in chess history can identify the players and figure out their personality on the basis of the moves played. In literature, just a couple of pages of a book are enough to tell the expert who wrote them, just as a single passage in a film reveals the director. Goethe claimed that he could tell which passages Schiller had written when drunk.

Two young people were holding hands at a side table, speaking a language I did not recognize. A couple seated further off were playing cards. Evidently they no longer had anything to say to one another. In his old age, my father would spend whole evenings playing patience in front of the TV. It looked like a miserable way to pass the hours, and I hoped that I would never sink so low.

The waiter brought me a fork and knife. They did not match, which suited the spirit of the place. My salad had chunks of goat cheese heaped on slices of rye bread, which looked crunchy, just like home. Hidden among lettuce leaves were radishes, onion slices and olives. A carrot was cut into the shape of the petals of a flower. I liked vegetables, but I did not want to turn into one.

Sampling the dark red wine, I thought about my Georgian pianist friend who had just given a concert at home. She had told me she practised at least five hours a day. If she did not, she could hear it in her playing, and soon so would the audience. She made up excuses to postpone sitting down at her grand piano, but as soon as she played the first notes, she was carried away by the music. This called for the same kind of dedication as top-level chess. Although pianists only play against themselves, they bring their listeners joy and energy.

There was something familiar about the woman at the back. I felt a thrill. She was the young lady who had sat opposite me on the train back from Jurmala. Her image had lodged itself in my brain.

She was sitting in a relaxed pose, twirling a lock of hair around her finger. Eyeing her furtively, I spilt some wine on the tablecloth. I covered the stain with a napkin. I leaned back in my chair, taking my time before attacking my salad. I wanted to create an impression of belonging there, of always arriving at the same time, stopping to catch my breath, swirling the velvety wine in my glass, and thinking elevated thoughts.

She took out a pencil and a notepad from her handbag. Glancing at me every once in a while, she drew a stroke or two, then examined the result, head askew. When our eyes met, she smiled in the same way as at the train station. If Igors had not gone to hospital, I would never have got a second chance.

The hand holding the pencil moved back and forth, stopped for a moment, then made curving motions. Whenever she took a break, she turned the pencil around between her lips. Riitta, my desk mate at school, on whom I had a crush, had a yellow pencil just like that, with an eraser at the head. When we were weighed on the first day of elementary school, we had to undress and stand side by side, naked.

I realized that she was drawing my portrait. Perhaps this was her way of making a move. I nibbled at my salad as if in a dream. I impaled a radish and chewed it slowly. The wine in my glass dwindled down, but I did not have the nerve to order more.

When I had finished my meal, I picked up a Latvian newspaper on the window sill and pretended to read the first page. It sported a photo from an ice hockey match in which Latvia had defeated Canada 2–0. Strangely enough, there had been no sign of the host country's victory being celebrated in the streets.

The woman came up to me and handed me her drawing.

– May I sit at your table? she asked in English.

– With pleasure.

I thanked her for the drawing, which was a rough and approximate sketch. Nonetheless, the figure holding a wineglass was clearly recognizable and characteristic. I liked it, unlike my reflection in the window of the shoe shop. I asked her to sign it.

– You look a little like Hemingway. Your glasses are like Brecht's.

– I don't have the vices to be Hemingway.

She noticed the cover of my book, and said that Čaks was a well-loved poet in Latvia, but not to everyone's taste. He had dedicated one of his poems to 'Stalin's organ', the Red Army's grenade launcher. Riga had Čaks's home museum as well as a monument to him in a nearby park.

I bookmarked the page with the feather in my pocket and put the book in my bag. She wore no makeup; her eyes were alert and her smile was contagious, creating a sense of intimacy. She wore an Indian-style dress and shawl, as well as a cloth bracelet inlaid with beads that looked like buckshot. Her fingernails were painted turquoise. The earring with a butterfly motif was the one she had worn on the train.

– Vilma, she said, and held out her hand.

– Matti, I replied. It's my pen name.

169

– It means 'hair' in Latvian.

– In Finnish it's the final position in chess, 'the death of the King'.

The waiter came over to collect my plate, glanced at me and said something to Vilma in Latvian. The card-playing couple were leaving. Pink Floyd blared from the speakers.

Vilma said she had seen me playing in Vērmanes Park. She had worked out that I was new in that youthful company. She had already guessed on the train that I was no local. She had wanted to ask me, but had been too shy to do so.

– Your T shirt had a picture of Che Guevara and some text in Spanish, Vilma said. What did it say?

– "As Governor of the Central Bank of Cuba, I learned nothing about banking".

– I didn't know he'd held that position.

– He was the only man to raise his hand when the rebels were looking for someone among them to lead the bank.

– No need for headhunters then. Why that text?

– In my former life, I worked for a central bank. As a foot soldier.

– *A propos*, how did you wind up among chess players?

I said I had come to Riga to meet grandmaster Igors Rausis, but had not known how to get in touch with him. One of the players in the park had given me a clue that led me to the shack where Rausis was working as a nightwatchman. I already knew that he was seriously ill.

– Did you find out what his illness was?

– A brain tumour.

I told her about my own illness. Before my trip, I had hoped that I could keep my fear of death at bay by studying and playing chess obsessively. I had thought that I would be able to breathe more freely in Riga, as it was a new city for me.

Vilma frowned, leaned back in her chair, and crossed her hands on top of her head. I could see in her eyes that she had her doubts about this kind of relief. She was on the verge of speaking, but held her tongue.

I told her about Rausis's chess career and the photo showing him sitting in the toilet with a mobile phone in his hand. I had had a desperate need to find out what it was all about. If he had been a banker caught for fraud, I would not have troubled my head with the matter. The association of deceit with the royal game and the resulting public uproar and sanctions had riled me.

Vilma had heard of the case, but she was not familiar with the details, and knew nothing about his illness. She said she had wondered how the affair had affected Rausis's life. Latvia was a small country, and there was no way of evading the blame and shame.

– It's possible to get to the summit of Mount Everest by helicopter, Vilma said. But is there any joy in it?

– Perhaps there is, if your friends applaud you and only the pilot knows the truth.

Vilma said that even as a child, she was captivated by the sight of the men playing in Vērmanes park. The fountains, statues, birds and sea of flowers also fascinated her. Sometimes a brass band played marches on the bandstand, or there was folk dancing. When the first snow covered the ground, she lay down on her back to make a snow angel. She could see where a hare had passed by, or where a hawk had eaten a pigeon. Snow lanterns and enormous carrot-nosed snowmen turned the park into a fairytale setting.

– Some people see winter as sweet summer's grave, but not me, Vilma said.

– Winter is a wonderful season, but Berlin has no proper winter.

– There's no guarantee of one in Riga either anymore.

Vilma knew that some of the men had played chess for money. There was a story that Mikhail Tal, the Wizard of Riga, had played in Vērmanes as a schoolboy and lost the money his mother had given him to buy ice cream.

– By the way, you can get ice cream here, too, Vilma said.

– Later perhaps.

Vilma thought time-worn wooden chess sets were as beautiful as jewellery. She would have liked to buy a set and to play too, but no one had taken the trouble to teach her. Her parents had thought chess was too difficult for children, and futile to boot.

In her student days, she bought a plastic set for two rubles in a bric-à-brac shop. She borrowed a chess guide for beginners from the library, and learned the moves and some opening variations.

When Latvia became independent, she travelled to Paris with a friend. They played chess for hours on the train. When they arrived, they continued playing next to the fountain in the Parc du Luxembourg. Vilma had just obtained her master's degree in cinematography.

Ah, Paris, Paris. I told her that I had been to Paris for meetings of the OECD financial markets committee. I prepared for the meetings by reading descriptions of Paris by Finnish writers.

At the dawn of my new life after leaving the bank, I had held my first photography exhibition in the heart of the Latin Quarter. The photos depicted a vanishing way of life in the Finnish backwoods. On the morning following the opening, I stood on the hill of Sacré Coeur with a hangover, gazing at the pearl-grey buildings and roofs disappearing into a haze. The whole scene felt like a stage set designed for my benefit.

– Same city, different experience, Vilma said.

Her chess studies after Paris had been desultory. Her enthusiasm for the game was rekindled when she mustered up the courage to watch the games in the park and pondered the players' strategies.

To learn more, she studied the games of the masters of the past.

One spring day, she sat at the stone board in the park, checking out on her smartphone moves played by chess legends, reproducing the moves with the real pieces. This made the games easier to follow than on the small screen.

A man passing by stopped to examine a position and challenged her to a game. After this, they played chess regularly. Playing chess enthralled Vilma and helped her forget her everyday worries, and to face them as well. Her chess strength improved rapidly.

Their relationship evolved beyond the game, and they moved in together, in retrospect too soon and on flimsy grounds. The relationship ended after some harrowing episodes, and she also stopped playing chess.

– Chess is not a strong enough glue to hold a relationship together, Vilma said.

– What was the problem?

– He started drinking. After the first flush of passion, our lovemaking began to feel like a business negotiation.

– What should it be like?

– One would hope for it to reveal hidden depths of personality.

After they broke up, Vilma did not want to touch the pieces again. Chess had been polluted by her traumatic experience. As for the friend Vilma had played with in Paris, she had known him since they were children. He preferred men, and her games with him were just chess, even though they slept in the same room in a *pension* near the Place de Stalingrad.

A man entered the café and gave Vilma a hug. He noticed the drawing on the table, glanced at me and said something to Vilma in Latvian. When he went to the other end of the room, Vilma said he was a classmate and that he had thought the drawing accurate, although it was just a rough sketch.

– His straw hat looks like a frayed lampshade, I said.

– He's an egghead with a brilliant future behind him.

– What went wrong?

– Stage fright.

I told her about a German woman who had watched me play chess at my usual café. When the game ended, the lady introduced herself as an actor and said she wanted to play me. Our relationship had also developed beyond chess. She had not recovered from her mother's recent death, and had hysterical fits which she blamed on me. That was the end of our association.

– How did your games with her go? Vilma asked.

– She thought about her moves for ages. It was a sheer waste of time.

– Did you tell her that?

– Indirectly. She was offended.

– An insoluble equation, Vilma said.

The same opening gambit had occurred once with a younger woman. We played blitz games, winning alternately. Between games, we told each other our life stories. Anna was studying to be a mechanical engineer, and also taught modern dance. She bubbled with high spirits and had a passion for chess, just like me. She had everything it takes to become a top player. I could have been her grandfather; there was no erotic spark between us, but we became friends. Creatures like her were created to light up the lives of old men like me, but also to torment us.

– Anna said she would never bind herself to another person.

– More and more people are saying that, Vilma said.

– Do you believe in marriage for life?

– Anyone who's afraid of solitude had better avoid marriage, Vilma said. How about you?

A partner can be like the moon in the sky. You know that it is there, even though you do not see it every day. Among the couples I knew among my own generation, only a handful appeared to be happy together. Some continued to plague one another even after divorce. At best, the life shared by couples seemed numbingly pleasant; at worst, marriage was a form of torture in which the spouses stayed together for fear of being left alone, losing face or having to adapt to a lower standard of living. If they were unlucky, these fears were compounded. Candlelit dinners did not help.

A fiftyish couple I once knew acted as if they had just fallen in love. It was a delight to see their happiness, for I knew it was genuine. Soon after our last meeting, the husband died of an aggressive pancreatic cancer. He was human in the best sense of the word. It often seemed to me that such people are taken away prematurely, whereas crooks keep thriving.

Some people looked to marriage to provide a safe haven in an evil world. Others surrendered their own identity. A colleague of mine took a keen interest in the history and culture of St Petersburg, and even learned Russian for the purpose. He never visited Leningrad or St Petersburg: his wife refused to travel to Russia. Even the tentacles of an octopus are capable of independent decisions.

After my mother died, my father was completely lost. They had barely taken a single step without each other; now they held hands in the tomb. Their life together had been sweet to observe, but frightening at the same time.

– Would you like to have something else? the waiter asked.

– A carafe of the same red wine, please, I said.

Vilma said the TV miniseries *The Queen's Gambit* had provided the decisive impulse for her to immerse herself in chess again. Her curiosity was initially aroused by the fact that the principal character, Beth, is a woman. Beth's dedication to chess makes her a new kind of role model.

Beth grows up in an orphanage, and her life is traumatic from the start. She later becomes involved in emotional entanglements, drugs and drinking. However, she remains sane thanks to chess and the support of her closest friends. She is able to participate successfully in major chess tournaments.

According to Vilma, the series is primarily an ode to friendship. If there was something she believed in, it was friendship. In the Soviet period, however, the word had taken on a hollow ring: 'friendship between peoples' was a hoax to cover up a ruthless struggle for power. Heads of state discussed 'questions of mutual interest'; that is, nothing.

– That's right, the kiss between Brezhnev and Honecker didn't send any trouser buttons flying, I said.

– They didn't even get as far as a French kiss, Vilma said.

Vilma said she had been moved to tears by the final scene in *The Queen's Gambit*. While the CIA is trying to groom Beth as a symbol of the free world in the Cold War, she slips off to cheers from a group of women to a boulevard lined with chess tables with fur-hatted old men sitting at them. The Muscovites recognize the young woman dressed in white who has just beaten the world champion, and rush to congratulate her. One of the men asks Beth to sit down opposite him. Beth takes off her white gloves, looks him in the eye and says, *Sygrayem*, let's play.

I told her I had heard that many shops ran out of chess sets because of *The Queen's Gambit*. It also made what was seen as a nerds' game go viral on the internet. The final scene had been shot in Berlin's Karl-Marx-Allee. The illusion was so credible that when watching I did not recognize the street, the erstwhile Stalin-Allee, although it should have been very familiar to me.

Inspired by the series, Vilma went to a flea market and bought an old set of wooden pieces and a board made of varnished birch, similar to those she had seen as a child. The wear and tear of the pieces seemed to link her to a chain of unknown chess players. She gazed at the set admiringly, like Henry Miller in his *Book of Friends*. The pieces, too, longed for the touch of a human hand again.

I told them how the pieces I had been given as a child became sentient beings to me, like objects in a fairytale by Hans Christian Andersen. It was sad to see them captured and pushed off the board, although that was part of the game. The large, decorative pieces remained engraved in my memory. Around the same time, I happened to see a scary poster advertising Ingmar Bergman's film *The Seventh Seal*.

– Chess was also a key theme in that film, I said.

– How so?

A mediaeval knight encounters Death on a deserted beach. The knight challenges Death to a game, and proposes that if he wins, Death will grant him more time. He tells Death about his dreams of what he would still like to achieve. Death agrees to play.

Death wins the game by delivering mate, and asks the knight whether he has done anything meaningful in his life. The knight replies in the affirmative. At the end, the Grim Reaper leads the knight and his retinue over the hills in a dance of death.

My illness made this scene seem even more macabre. If I were to meet Death, I would propose the same deal as the knight, and for the same reason. I would also make the same reply to Death's question. In this game, I would not be able to afford a single mistake. I knew from experience that just one bad move could cancel out dozens of good ones.

In his memoirs, Bergman wrote that for him, mustering the courage to present death as a figure who talked and played chess with people was a step in his personal struggle to overcome the fear of dying. He never feared death again after that film. I thought his struggle credible and heartening.

– The purpose of art is to prepare people for death, Vilma said.

I told her about the mediaeval church of Täby near Stockholm, which contains a mural by Albertus Pictor showing Death playing chess. Bergman probably got the idea for the chess game in *The*

Seventh Seal from this painting.

Vilma told me she had heard a song by Scott Walker called *The Seventh Seal*. The lyrics were based on Bergman's film. *This morning I played chess with Death, said the knight. We played that he might grant me time…*

She knew that most of the games at the top level were drawn. A draw was not a possible outcome in a game against Death.

– In Walker's song, the knight accuses Death of cheating, Vilma said.

– I can't remember any such accusation in the film, I said.

– Death has no reason to cheat.

– Igors had several reasons, and he feared the reverse accusation, I said.

– Perhaps he himself didn't know why he did what he did.

– That's what I think, too.

Igors had said that getting caught in Strasbourg had saved his life. Until then, he had avoided the most strenuous treatments, as they would have affected his playing decisively. The treatments had bought him more time, though, as his wife Ajgul put it, with reduced content.

Nonetheless, even as he sought to justify his actions, he was ashamed of them. At the age of thirty, he had been close to joining the world elite. Now that he was sixty, he had accepted the thought of death, but he refused to accept that it was not possible to keep playing at the same level, let alone to improve. His illness had impaired his physical fitness, which was a problem in long games played for hours on end.

Perhaps he identified with the Russian grandmaster Viktor Korchnoi, who was still among the 100 best players in the world at the age of 75. Even when he was over 80 years old and had just recovered from a stroke, Korchnoi still played and defeated another grandmaster. A feat like this would not be possible for someone who had grown up in the world of computer chess. Perhaps it would not be possible for anyone else either. Today's rising young stars play with machine-like accuracy, giving them a decisive edge.

Vilma said that our ulterior motives often remain obscure; moreover, quite possibly they are not really what we say they are. Sometimes one may be tempted to attempt the impossible. A self-image that matches hopes with reality is a sign of maturity, whereas they may have been out of sync in the later years of Igors's chess career.

Speaking of Bergman's films, Vilma said she had recently seen *Wild Strawberries*. Its plot also centres on death and transience. An old professor drives to the university town of Lund to receive an honorary doctorate. On the way there, he realizes that his life is a lie: his research has made him neglect human relationships, and he has become an embittered old man.

At the end of the film, the professor's travel companions take him to a sunny clearing on the banks of a lake. There he regains a flicker of his youthful enthusiasm. The story is gloomy, but Vilma said she had sensed a hint of peace in the final scene.

– It's a Chekhovian film, I said.

The waiter brought a carafe and a box of salted nuts to our table and said the nuts were on the house. She wiped the neighbouring table clean and watered the red geranium on the window sill. The granny flower looked out of place in this setting. No doubt the effect was intentional.

I filled our glasses and said I had once played the role of the Grim Reaper. I bought a scythe with a wooden handle at a Helsinki flea market and carried it to the office on my shoulder during the morning rush hour, intending to take it home after work. The sight both frightened and amused passers-by, but no one said a word. Only a vagrant sprawling on a park bench commented.

– Oh hell, not yet! he cried.

– That would make a good subject for a short film, Vilma said.

She told me she taught cinematography and looked at everyday situations from a filmmaker's perspective. She had made films of her own and had also written scripts. She was in her dream profession. Her career choice had already been foreshadowed by childhood theatre games, which she filmed with a wooden cine camera. Her parents observed her antics with amusement, but did not encourage her to embark on a career in film. She never became the happy tank driver of the song she had had to sing in kindergarten.

Her training had taught her to watch films analytically, which made it difficult to be enraptured by them. Yet if a film, such as *Wild Strawberries*, was powerful enough, she was able to immerse herself in the narrative flow. Occasionally the same thing happened with some random syrupy soap opera.

– By the way, what were you reading on the train? I asked.

– A list of classic love scenes in film.

– Whatever for?

– I was making it for an American movie director.

– What does he need it for?

– As background for a film of her own. She wants to avoid sugariness and is studying ways to depict love in films by the great masters.

Vilma said she had visited film archives to see how directors created love scenes by cinematic means, how they directed the expressions, gestures, movements and speech of actors and what kind of images and editing solutions they used to construct scenes and sequences.

– Well, what did you discover?

– Love eludes definitions and generalizations. At its best, it forms a bridge between sensuality and spirituality.

Vilma considered *Hiroshima Mon Amour* by Alain Resnais to be the most moving romance film of all. In it, a French woman and a Japanese man meet in a city burnt to cinders. In the course of one night, they open up to one another about their lives, and fall passionately in love. The film made her forget everything Hollywood had taught her about narration and time.

The man who had been playing chess was now writing down mathematical formulas in an exercise book. They gave me the creeps. In a regular dream I had, I was threatened with losing my master's degree and my pension because I had failed a compulsory repeat exam in mathematics. I had forgotten how to solve second-degree equations.

Pink Floyd had given way to Led Zeppelin: and the forest will echo with laughter... When Vilma came back from the bathroom, she touched my hair lightly. Munching nuts, I told her about meeting and playing chess with Gustav in Vērmanes Park. He had got to know Igors in hospital. Although they were from different walks of life, their personalities had clicked. Gustav had liver cancer, which he considered a fair price to pay for the joys of vodka.

– I didn't know what to say to that.

– Everyone makes their own choices, and hopefully understands the consequences, Vilma said.

Gustav realized that his steps were getting shorter and twilight was at hand, but he did not want to waste what remained of his life on the fear of death. To that extent, he and Igors were kindred spirits. I could not tell whether their world was so constructed that they would not go back in time even if they could.

Vilma said she used to walk across the park every day. The chess players projected a sweet sense of brotherhood. Most of them were aged, but they did not give the impression of just waiting for the end. Their winters must seem endlessly long.

There was not a single woman among the players. Vilma said she wanted to be the first one, but only when she was good enough to match their skill. Otherwise they would talk behind her back about that poor girl who only has a vague notion of the game and is out of her depth.

I told her that most of the statues in the park were of men, although that was not a Vērmanes specialty. True, on the edge of the park I had photographed a statue of three naked women holding hands.

– It's a pretty work of art, Vilma said.

– Wasn't female nudity frowned on in the Soviet period?

– Someone had the idea of calling the statue *Peace Dance*.

– *Lesbian Dance* would have been rejected, I said.

I told her about Judit Polgár of Hungary, one of the few women among the top players. She became a grandmaster at the age of fifteen, and was No. 8 in the world in her prime. She was known as a brilliant attacking player.

Garry Kasparov once said that chess was not for women because their psyche was not equipped to deal with long games. They should concentrate on raising children instead. He retracted his words when Judit beat him in the Russia vs. The World match in 2002.

– Judit is another great example for you, in addition to Beth, I said.

– What induced her to play chess?

– Italian vanilla ice cream.

– Ice cream?

Judit's father László Polgár was a Hungarian chess teacher and author. He had two other daughters besides Judit. According to Igors, László was not a particularly strong player, but he was well-versed in theories of chess. According to László, there were no born geniuses; you could only become a genius with proper coaching.

László started preparing his daughters to become chess masters before their third birthday. He took them out of school and homeschooled them. They loved ice cream, especially the Italian ice cream sold from a kiosk in the centre of Budapest. He gave them chess problems to solve, and whenever they managed to solve one, he bought them an ice cream.

– Sounds a bit like Pavlov's dogs, Vilma said.

– He succeeded, but hardly without inflicting any social damage.

When I played my East German colleague in the Széchenyi baths in Budapest, we stood in the water with the board on the edge of the pool, steam swirling up all around. We were not the only chess players there, but not one of them was a woman.

Of course the weight of tradition is strong. There were only a handful of girls among Igors's pupils. I said I had wondered about whether this was the explanation for the superiority of men at chess. It was a sensitive subject that could easily land you in deep water.

Igors had said he had enjoyed *The Queen's Gambit*, although he had thought it a pretty fairytale and the picture that it painted of a female player's chances was too rosy. He said that for hormonal reasons men had a stronger urge to take risks, and this was crucial in the decisive stages of the game. Echoing Kasparov, Igors said that women were also more likely to tire at the end of a six-hour game, leading to mistakes.

Vilma said that women think, feel and act differently from men. Even their attitude to the pieces is different. She hoped to discover at Vērmanes how, if at all, this affects their play. In any case, it was nonsense to generalize that reason and rationality are typically male characteristics and emotions and irrationality female ones.

– How strong are the players in the park? Vilma asked.

– Not master level, but the best of them are close.

The old men had persevered with chess for decades. They were dilettantes in the original sense of the word, taking delight in the game; they were familiar with the game's basic principles and essential opening theory. Most of them played blitz, which is ruled by the clock. I could not tell how good they were at classical chess; in some ways, the two are different games.

Pieces that look unusual or have odd shapes have always given me trouble. In one set I had played with, a missing pawn had been replaced with a champagne cork painted black. I was emotionally attached to my own set: the pieces seemed to anticipate my moves. Some great chess players of the past had also felt that the pieces had a will of their own and wished to occupy squares on which they felt comfortable. They said this wish should be respected.

I said that as a child I had studied the games reproduced in chess books while trying to imagine what the players had been thinking at key moments. More recently, I had learned a great deal about top-level chess from online commentary by experienced players assisted by computer analysis. How far I could have advanced with proper training from an early age remained a mystery.

– I don't know if I was lucky or unfortunate that it didn't happen.

– What's past is past.

Even if the houses around the park had collapsed, the chess players in the park probably would not have noticed anything. This experience alone would have made my visit to Riga worthwhile. In Paris, I had watched old men in berets playing pétanque. Under the plane trees, they puffed at their cigars, talking little; all that could be heard was the chirping of sparrows, the scraping of sand and the clinking of boules.

In supermarket lobbies back home, I had seen pensioners standing alone in front of slot machines or lottery counters. That was one way of awaiting the end – in Finland, the world's happiest country.

The films of Aki Kaurismäki had made Vilma wonder what it meant to be Finnish. She had been particularly moved by a scene in which a man sitting at a bar takes a used teabag out of his pocket and drops it into a cup of boiling water brought by the bartender.

I said Aki may have wanted to show that such things could happen, and sometimes did. His films express an undying nostalgia for a country that no longer exists – and yet continues to exist, and with which I identify. The films are fairytales for adults, and telling these tales is the purpose of his life.

Vilma said she had sensed Aki's dedication to his craft: Let's hope he doesn't keep his promise to stop making movies. If he does continue, however, he should avoid repetition. As they grow older, many directors make films that look too much like themselves.

For my part, I hoped that Aki would avoid the sermons that undermined the political message in some of his films. My chess friend Gustav was a Kaurismäki character. He was who he was, proudly and with his head held high. He said that there was no longer any reason for pessimism once the game was lost. All he wanted to take with him to the grave was a chess set, the shreds of his FC Caramba Riga football shirt and a bottle of Stolichnaya vodka, from which he would offer the first swig to St Peter at heaven's gate.

I had my first taste of Stolichnaya in Leningrad half a century ago. I was staying at the Hotel Astoria, where Hitler had intended to celebrate his conquest of the city. I spent the morning watching chess players in the Summer Park by the River Neva. Old men in dark clothes stood motionless next to the tables. A bottle of vodka did the rounds. One of the men shifted his cap to shield himself from the sun, another lit a hand-rolled *makhorka*. White marble statues shone in the background, as if expecting to be invited to play a game. As it happens, many of them depicted female figures.

Watching the games, I lost my sense of time and melted into the summer haze. I half hoped Alexander Pushkin would interrupt his morning stroll to join the crowd, the hem of his nightshirt flapping.

Already then, I had taken a fancy to Anton Chekhov's notion that there is no happiness that is not idleness, and only what is unnecessary is pleasurable. Chess was not necessary, or if it was, only to a few people. Because of my illness, however, idleness now savoured of time wasted.

Chekhov and Igors lived in different centuries, but I had toyed with the idea that they meet in Yalta, and Chekhov goes on to write a short story inspired by Igors's chess career. Instead of a moralizing sermon, it becomes a lively portrayal of the complexity of the human mind, against the background of the fragilities in Anton's own life.

– Why not, though what a writer writes and what a writer thinks about life are two different things, Vilma said.

I proposed a toast to the memory of my beloved Chekhov. In my youth, a friend gave me a pair of portrait photographs, one of which depicted Chekhov and the other myself retouched in period style. With this gift, my friend hoped to encourage me to keep writing.

Vilma said she had visited Chekhov's villa in Yalta, which had been turned into a museum. It was a dreamy place to spend one's waning days, or would have been, had they not been overshadowed by his failing lungs and impending death.

– Speaking of failing lungs, do you smoke? I asked.

– I sometimes take a drag to steady my nerves.

– I smoked the first cigarette of my life earlier this evening. And the last.

I did not feel that I had missed out on some supernatural delight. I took the tin box out of my pocket and handed it to Vilma.

– I was wondering where I'd lost that, she said.

– I found it on the floor of the Jurmala train.

– The odyssey of a cigarette case.

– And its happy return home.

I said I did not know whether Chekhov's lung troubles were brought on by smoking, but I did know he had written a monologue about its dangers. Nor did I know whether Anton played chess. Pushkin did. Chess was a duel but not a mortal one. Pushkin was grateful to his wife for learning the game. I said both writers lived on in their books. Chess grandmasters sacrificed their lives to a game that left no permanent mark on the world.

In Igors's experience, as he got closer to the top in chess, his love of the game gradually withered, the joy of playing diminished and the danger of a fall grew. The fear of losing his strength and the austerity of the lifestyle increase the danger. The philosopher Diderot had told François Philidor that it was madness to run the risk of becoming an imbecile through vanity. Philidor was the best player in the world for the better part of the 18th century. Among the opponents he played were Voltaire and Rousseau, both of whom he defeated effortlessly.

Towards the end of his life, Philidor became delusional and feared being robbed of his shoes so that he would have to walk barefoot. By that time, Diderot was no longer around to say I told you so.

In the following century, Paul Morphy became champion of the United States. According to Igors, Morphy played chess obsessively. For Morphy, the ability to play chess was the sign of a gentleman, but the ability to play chess well was the sign of a wasted life. Igors suspected that the reason for Morphy's disparaging remark was that a lady had rejected his proposal of marriage on the grounds that he was only a chess player. At the end of Morphy's life, his mental health deteriorated.

I had read about Morphy's contemporary Wilhelm Steinitz, who became world champion in the latter half of the 19th century and is considered the "Father of Modern Chess". Steinitz later invented an invisible telephone that he used to call his friends. When they did not answer, he called God and challenged him to a match, offering him odds of a pawn.

– The story of Bobby Fischer is widely known, I said.

– Beth's rise to the top in *Queen's Gambit* is loosely based on Fischer's career, Vilma said.

– But they didn't want the TV series to end badly like Fischer's life, I said.

– It was an American series.

I had heard that one grandmaster had called chess a depressive game: the pain of losing was greater than the joy of victory. Gamblers knew that experience. For the few chess players who had won the world championship, the tens of thousands of hours they had spent at the board may not have seemed like a complete waste of time.

Champion swimmers train by swimming from one end of the pool to the other for hours on end. Vilma said some of them use jabs and pills to gain more speed. To an outsider, the whole business looks masochistic, but who knows what goes on in a swimmer's head? A single injury can undo years of training. Once their career is over, many sink into a void.

When you are at the top, there is only one way to go. Vilma said an Oriental creed states that when you reach the summit, you must keep climbing, eventually disappearing from view.

The woman sitting at the table next to ours had nibbled at her salad and left the rest. I said I had learned as a child that you have to eat what is put on your plate, but I did not wish to judge these modern young people. However, I had once asked jokingly if I could eat the rest.

– Are you hungry? I asked.

– I ate at home before leaving.

– I wish I'd found this place on my first evening in Riga.

– Well, now you know about it.

Paolo, an artist friend of mine, had come close to the top in chess. For him, playing chess was a way to practise patience and concentration and cope with life's problems. This meant that there were no winners. He immersed himself in game positions as a form of meditation, paying no attention to his opponent or to the result of the game. Facing an arrogant opponent, however, would arouse his killer instinct, and then winning became the object of the game.

When I played with Paolo, he pointed out every inferior move I made during the game, told me to take it back and showed me better options. After the games, he would analyse the key moments. I told Vilma that these games had been lessons for me, just like my games with Igors. They had always left me in a good mood.

Paolo told me he once played the Armenian grandmaster Levon Aronian, who was world No. 2 at the time. During the game, Paolo had a panic attack and had to resign. He said Aronian came from another universe, and did not want to play him again.

I told Paolo that I wanted to retain the joy of the game, and was therefore content to remain a club-level player. Even as a child, I had feared that my playing would get out of hand. Of course it was gratifying to be able to raise my level at this age. The same would not be possible for grandmasters, since their level was already so high.

I had also learned from Igors that though many players had become masters, no one had been able to master chess, let alone their own life. Anyone who claimed otherwise understood nothing. The most important lesson I had learned from Igors was how to confront illness and death. In his words, chess was only a game, and there was no point in living for it alone. The paradox was that his own life had been devoted solely to chess.

– Life is full of paradoxes, Vilma said.

– Igors's life in particular.

I had also become aware in Igors's shack that the obsessive playing triggered by my cancer diagnosis was problematical. What difference did it make whether my rating was one hundred points higher or lower? It would never be recorded in my book of achievements. At least Igors had a financial incentive to maintain his position at the top.

Vilma said she had immediately had the same thought, but had not found a tactful way to broach the topic. Chess is a limited, predictable space consisting of just 64 squares. The players sit in a hermetic cosmos, whereas life is unpredictable and limitless. Even in the final stretch, one would hope for life to prevail over chess. This was what she had thought when reading *The Luzhin Defence* by Nabokov. It had made her vaguely restless. The games played in Vērmanes Park scarcely had anything in common with Luzhin's world.

Nabokov once said in an interview that of all the novels he had written in Russian, *The Luzhin Defence* contained and diffused the most warmth. The book was loved even by readers who had no understanding of chess and were unimpressed by his other novels. Even the fact that the protagonist jumps out of the window at the end evidently did not put them off.

During his years in Germany, Nabokov composed chess problems for newspapers. He was also a butterfly researcher of international renown. He arrived in Berlin as a stateless refugee. There he reassessed the basis of his life and his relationship to language. I had done the same, so I was in good company in Berlin.

The waiter cleared the dishes from the neighbouring table and asked me where I was from. When I told her, she said Sunrise Avenue was her favourite band. I boasted that Finland was a great power in music: according to the great Finnish film director Aki Kaurismäki, Finnish sailors had brought the tango to Argentina, from where it had spread all over the world.

Vilma thought that my account of Gustav dying of liver cancer was moving. He would play chess as long as he could, and depart without a murmur when his time was up. That was as it should be. The game was probably not so much an escape for him as part of his daily routine.

– You make it all sound so simple, I said.

– It's easier to philosophize about death than to face it.

I said I had watched the final scene of the film *La diagonale du fou* (Dangerous Moves) on the web. An old chess master lies in bed in intensive care. A former opponent of his, still a young man, comes to play one last game with the patient, who is dying of heart disease. They play without board or pieces, each player announcing his move in turn. This was not the kind of final act I wanted, nor did I think Gustav would, even though he said he had played blindfold chess in his time.

I said I had sometimes wondered how it was possible for chess geniuses to play up to ten blindfold games simultaneously. Some masters had experienced the force fields of chess in their original purity when the board was stripped of tangible pieces.

Igors only played anti-poetic internet chess these days, and fitfully at that. Even there, the feeling of shame sometimes overcame him. Ajgul still blamed him for cheating, and rejected her husband's pretext that he had been seeking salvation by obeying a higher will.

I did not know what Igors saw when looking in the mirror in the morning. His humiliation in Strasbourg had not blighted him, and he seemed to have retained his integrity better than many top players who considered themselves honest. He did not show any sign of bitterness. Igors had performed a dishonest act honestly, or at least that was the impression he managed to convey.

Igors's last opponent had died of brain cancer soon after the Strasbourg tournament. During the tournament, they had not been aware that they shared the same fate.

– Igors was tormented by his opponent's death, I said.

– Even though it wasn't his fault, Vilma said.

– He couldn't explain the feeling.

– The human conscience is a mystery. What we cannot explain, we must pass over in silence.

Igors would no doubt keep teaching children chess for the rest of his life; it was his destiny. Children never judged him. He had told me that if he had worries before facing his class, they all disappeared when he was coaching. His eyes lit up as he spoke in a way that was unmistakably genuine.

– Does Igors have any dreams left? Vilma asked.

– A few, but they will remain dreams. He thinks brooding is a waste of time.

– A sensible attitude.

When the ban was over, however, Igors still intended to play in senior tournaments. He could regain his grandmaster title by winning the title of senior world champion, the world's best over 65-year-old. He knew making a comeback would be difficult; when playing internet chess, he had noticed that he had become slower and had lost his strong awareness of time. On the other hand, the same surely went for other senior players, too. Nonetheless, I considered his notion of becoming world champion to be a pipe dream. Perhaps his optimism would protect him, regardless of whether it was justified.

– Justified or not, we live on hope, Vilma said.

It seemed to her that Igors had trusted me and that his opening up had done both of us good. It was like a Catholic confession. Thrashing out the confusion of existence among friends was the best therapy. The confusion was not resolved, but at least it became more acceptable.

I said Ajgul was wise and more clear-headed than her husband, but she knew little about the chess world. I suspected that Igors had no close friends with whom to discuss his career choices and who could have warned him about taking part in the tournament in Strasbourg under the influence of medication.

The first time that I fully realized how important such a friend can be was when my closest friend in Finland died. Whenever I was in a serious predicament, my first instinct was still to call him. Back in the 1970s, he had been within a hair's breadth of completing a doctoral thesis in literary criticism. He had showed me a draft list of people to invite to the afterparty. It stayed in his desk drawer. I suspect that he was overcome by stage fright. In contrast, Hitler had already had his invitations to the Hotel Astoria printed.

I would have new friends, but not of the kind with whom years shared formed a meaningful soundboard, and who could deduce all the information they needed from my expressions and gestures.

When Igors had showed me photographs of his family in his shack, he had said that the closer he came to his future – meaning the grave –, the more clearly he saw his past. I knew the feeling.

He also had photographs of chess events in various parts of the world, but not of the cities in which the tournaments had been played or where he had coached. When in Paris, I had photographed the streets, the people and the pigeons. I did not have a single shot of the venue for OECD meetings, with which I had become very familiar. This was a pity. I had later encouraged my friends to photograph their workplaces and everyday situations, to which only time can lend allure.

I showed Vilma two photos on my iPad. In one, Gustav was contemplating his next move with wrinkled brow; in the other, Igors was sitting in his shack, smiling. Discussing chess, Igors had spoken about the appreciation of beauty, but his shack was ascetic. It was Igors's monastic cell, whereas Vērmanes was Gustav's proletarian summer residence.

– Gustav looks as if he has escaped from a Kaurismäki film, Vilma said.

– Or a Gogol novel, I said. Aki loves characters like that.

– The shack could also be lifted straight out of one of Aki's films, Vilma said.

– Perhaps furnished with an official portrait of the President of Latvia.

I told her I had worried beforehand what Igors would make of a guest who turned up uninvited to interrogate him like a doctor interrogates a patient. I need not have worried: our meetings had been straightforward and rewarding. He had adopted a fatherly attitude towards me, even though I was older.

Igors's socialist ideals sounded congenial. I had avoided pointing out that they had turned into a travesty. However, he was no turncoat who switched flags and songs to please whoever was in power. I knew such people, some of them close acquaintances. They embellished their shifting allegiances by claiming to have changed perspective. Some thought their belief in socialism had justified even actions that later turned out to be errors.

Vilma said that many people equated socialism with their youth, gilded by memory. The political realities remained alien to them, whereas the settings, events and objects of their early years blended to form something that was more real than the twists and turns of history.

I told her about a friend of mine in East Berlin. Going on his first camping trip with a friend, he had bought a small box that held two boiled eggs, a tiny salt cellar and two spoons. The box later brought back the experiences of that trip vividly. The first snow falls every winter. Our first love is unique.

I had also bought a few of these red-and-yellow egg boxes. Holding the endearing little objects in my hand, I thought that the state that had produced them could not be all evil. I had also picked up other classic GDR products at flea markets, and had assembled a small home museum. Contemplating them, I mused about how I would have felt if the familiar products from my childhood in Finland had suddenly vanished from the shop shelves.

– We lived through that change in Latvia, Vilma said.

– Igors listened to his Spidola radio for sentimental reasons, even though it crackled.

Igors had told me about Alexandria, where his father had trained the crew of a fishing boat. After the ascetic life they had led in the Soviet Union, the fairytale street in which they lived and its cafés had seemed like a leap into another world. So had their return to Sevastopol.

Igors's years in Alexandria had been a key experience in his life. My own childhood had been completely different, but its significance was similar. I suspected that our meeting had been marked by the fellowship of two men nearing death. But I had not found a kindred spirit in him.

Occasionally, when two people meet, they have an overwhelming sense of community based on a similar sense of humour. This is a genuinely profound phenomenon. It is often trivialized into a notion of what different people find amusing. Igors told amusing stories, but that was different.

– The best humorists are not typically funny, Vilma said.

I did not know if I would ever meet Igors again. We will meet if God wills, he might say. I will try to hold on to my own will with two hands, to the end.

I poured more wine and we clinked glasses. Vilma took a sip and turned her eyes to the people in the street.

– I would like to make a documentary about the players in the park, she said.

– A good subject that opens up in many different directions, I said.

– Do you think they'd let me?

– I think they'd be flattered.

– Even though I'm a woman?

– They'd understand that wasn't your choice.

I told her what I had heard from a Georgian friend about the chess-playing women of her country who had become stars. One of them, Nona Gaprindashvili, was the first female grandmaster. A recent documentary film barely scratched the surface of the subject, but it did shed a light on the cult status these women enjoyed in their country. Many a girl had been named after them.

– I don't think the filmmakers knew much about the world of chess, I said.

– It's pretty bad when the director is unfamiliar with the subject, Vilma said.

– At least you're on the right path in that respect. You are curious, open to the world, and trying to improve your chess. The players can sense that.

– Thanks for the encouragement.

Vilma said that her idea also arose from practical observation. Such thoughts often bubbled up to the surface at night. She was fascinated by the jigsaw puzzle of observations, experiences and memories.

– How deeply have you thought about it?

She said she could already see the shape of the film in her mind's eye, meaning the general approach, a series of scenes or simply the emotional atmosphere. Making it happen would require trust, which meant the players would have to accept her as one of them. Gaining access was a fascinating challenge in itself.

Everything has been said and nothing is new in art, but Vilma thought a film – or any other work of art – can have an impact if it reflects the unique experiences of its author and sums up their feelings about life. Behind this notion were her memories of Vērmanes: subtle, lingering moments. She hoped to reawaken the viewer's own childhood memories. This was what had happened to her recently when she read Nathalie Sarraute's novel *L'Enfance*, although the childhood depicted in it had nothing to do with her own.

– There is magic in turning personal experiences into something universal, I said.

If you do not understand your own life, you are not likely to understand the actions of the characters you depict. Vilma wanted her film to reflect the poetry of the everyday, with which viewers would identify regardless of their familiarity with chess. She believed that the film could give new meaning to the viewer's own memories as well.

The risk lay in idealizing the situation. Perhaps some of the men were escaping a nagging wife or channelling their sexual urges into the game. The atmosphere might be tainted by linguistic or political tensions between players, or by tensions that remained hidden. These elements, too, would be part of the story. Discovering them would require time and patience, and the documentary format was no guarantee of success. Perhaps the film would eventually take a fictional turn.

In Soviet Latvia, the world had to be depicted idealistically, as it was assumed or hoped to be. For Vilma, this was a grotesque game in which the rules were known, although never written out as in chess. She wished to depict life as it was, without interpreting it.

Another option was to concentrate on one character, such as Gustav, and to tell the story through him. Gustav sounded like a charismatic figure who would not freeze in front of the camera.

First, however, she would have to delve deeper into the world of chess. Vilma asked me whether I could teach her the strategic finesses of the game and come to the park to lend her psychological support. Since the men already knew about the Finnish stranger, this would smooth her introduction.

– It's a tempting thought, but my return flight is tomorrow.

– Pity. Is it the last flight from Riga?

– Well, perhaps not…

The chairs were being piled up on the table and the floor was being swept. The waiter's expression signalled that it was time to pay the bill. She gave me a cardboard box for the drawing, and asked me to say hello to my sailors and to thank them on behalf of the world's tango lovers.

– Will do, I said. Compliments to your winemaker. He's in the right business.

Out in the deserted street, I took a deep breath of the cooling air. The wine had sharpened my senses and soothed the pain of living in a wicked world. My body felt light, as if gravity had weakened. The whole of creation seemed to merge and open up towards infinity.

I walked by Vilma's side, heedless of where we were going,

reliving the nocturnal perambulations of my youth, savouring the moment beyond time and place. Wherever our path was taking us, we were in no hurry to get there.

A sickle moon had risen above the roofs, and swifts circled in the sky. I said their flight appeared to express pure joy, although it was actually a struggle for survival against time. I preferred to look at birds through the eyes of a poet. Goethe's greatness was in how the scientist coexisted with the poet.

The notes of a Vivaldi cello concerto wafted from an open window. A white curtain fluttered in the wind. The cellist was invisible except for a flickering shadow on the wall. The plaster rosette on the ceiling brought to mind the symbol of the infinite universe. We stopped under the window.

Time stood still, and we forgot about its ebb. I said moments like this were a musical celebration. I hardly ever went to concerts. It was not something you did spontaneously; nor was it possible to escape the overpowering fragrance of the person sitting next to you.

The music stopped, and the cellist closed the window. Vilma glanced at her watch and realized that her last train had gone. She spotted a taxi at the other end of the street and hailed for it to stop.

Zolitūde, she said to the driver, mentioning the name of the street. He turned on the meter and made a U turn. I told Vilma I had had a glimpse of that suburb from the train window on my trip to Jurmala.

– Bonjour tristesse, I had thought as rows of houses among trees flashed past.

– It's certainly no Hipster Mecca, Vilma said with a grin.

We leaned against each other silently. I was overcome by a pleasant drowsiness. Her scent was lily of the valley. I thrilled to the soft touch of her hand. The rhythm of her breathing was faster than mine.

After crossing the Daugava bridge, the taxi zigzagged through a maze of low-rise housing. The driver sat behind a blurry plexiglass. He answered his phone in Russian, saying he would come home after this last ride, no doubt talking to his wife.

Last ride of the night, I thought. In my mind's eye, I saw a linen cloth attached to the porch wall in a deserted old house in North Karelia. It bore the embroidered inscription *God's mercies are new every morning*.

From the edge of a meadow, a shoreless sea of housing stretches out, buildings of varying height scattered higgledy-piggledy in the weedy field. In a deserted backyard, the ropes of a swing dangle from the frame, swaying in the wind. The swing's seat is missing. The window of a hairdresser's salon is covered by a poison-green lattice ravaged by rust.

– You can find lattices like this everywhere from the Baltic countries to Vladivostok, I say.

A flowering bird cherry tree grows in the yard, the only tree in the immediate vicinity. I sniff the white blossoms, picturing the bird cherry tree on my childhood island, likewise the only tree in sight. This specimen looks like an errant angel lost among tower blocks. If you forget your address, the angel will lead you back home.

I catch a familiar whiff of the Soviet Union in the stairway, perhaps a detergent. The lift clatters and shakes, reminding me of the Jurmala train. It stops at the top floor, the sixteenth.

– You find the house odd, Vilma says.

– *Back in the USSR, hey, you don't know how lucky you are*, I hum.

– We are architects of our own fortune, Vilma says.

– Up to a point.

– Quite.

Vilma says the house is no architectural masterpiece, but she is somehow pleased by its spareness. In rainy weather, moisture oozes from the joints between the building blocks, but the roof still holds the rain. The sound insulation is poor, but no matter: the neighbours are quiet folk.

The wall in the hallway is lined with botanical prints. Vilma says they were made by her grandfather based on plants he gathered and pressed. I tell her that collecting plants used to be an annual chore for schoolchildren during the summer holidays in Finland. We also had to learn their Latin names, which seemed like a pointless burden on the memory.

A cat is stretching itself and scratching its climbing frame. She comes over to sniff my hand.

– That's Anastasia's way of saying hello to new people, Vilma says.

– What breed is she?

– Russian Blue. She's from a pet orphanage in Kaliningrad.

– Why was she abandoned?

– Because of the light spot right there.

– Just because of one spot?

– It meant she couldn't take part in cat shows.

Vilma tells me that Anastasia often parks in front of the computer screen to hunt the cursor until Vilma takes a break to play with her. The independent spirit of cats has always appealed to Vilma. Pablo Neruda wrote that cats were born perfect, walking alone and knowing what they wanted. She remembered that idea when her traumatic relationship ended.

I say Neruda knew his cats. When comparing the horrors of capitalism with Soviet bliss, however, he wrote like a one-eyed political commissar.

A Berlin friend of mine also had a Russian Blue. She had promised her cat never to take her to a cat show again. Apparently the breed had been close to extinction because its fur was used for making warm caps for soldiers. In Gogol's short story *The Overcoat*, an official cannot afford to have the collar of his overcoat made of marten fur. He winds up choosing cat fur, which looks like marten from a distance. This was the first story I read in the original Russian.

I say that world champion Alekhine wanted to play with his lucky Siamese cat in his lap. Incidentally, he hoped his opponent might be allergic to cats. When the cat was banned, Alekhine started wearing a sweater with a picture of the cat on it.

Vilma's room contains a sofa that has seen better days, a blood-red folding table, and a floor lamp with a brass stand and three tulip-shaped opal reflector bowls. A bookshelf assembled from sturdy apple boxes contains novels, books about cinema and photography, and a few slim volumes, presumably of poetry. I restrain myself from examining the books.

The various items of furniture have probably come from a flea market. I imagine their stories, until subjectivity takes over. A ceramic pot containing a yucca palm rests on a birchwood block with drops of congealed resin on the surface, as if the tree is weeping its fate.

The walls are hung with pencil drawings and a wood-framed King Kong poster from the 1930s. On the table is a pile of papers; the top sheet has handwritten notes in the margin. A tablecloth with a lace fringe is adorned with large, curving initials sewn in red thread.

– Pretty tablecloth, I say.
– Initialled by my grandma.
– The spirit of your grandparents hovers over your home.

I pick up a tulip petal from the floor and rub it between my fingers. It has a lemony scent. The tulips have wilted, and are bent rather like the glass bowls at the tips of the lamp's brass branches. The bowls are decorated with a faint leaf pattern.

The window looks out on a panorama consisting of hundreds of similar windows. The bluish flicker of a TV set can still be seen in some of them. I feel as if I have landed in the middle of a Kieslowski film.

– This seems to be the tallest building in the neighbourhood, I say.

– It is, but that doesn't give me a sense of superiority.

– They've all been beheaded.

– The golden age of flat roofs.

Vilma says that when it snows, the gloomy scene is wrapped in a white mantle that lends it an unreal beauty. Looking out the window, one can barely distinguish the other seasons.

Zolitūde is a Russian stronghold. Vilma says she is planning to make a documentary on the area. The locals call it Zolik. They cannot afford a flat in the centre of town. Many say they like it here, and unlike what one might imagine, the gigantic scale of the buildings actually draws people together: you can sometimes hear them asking their neighbours – even complete strangers – for a box of matches or a plaster. They feel among their own here.

Vilma does not think of Zolitūde as her final stop, however: she longs to live by the seaside. She wants to buy a house in Jurmala, where she has friends. Anastasia will have her own enclosed yard there. The train trip provides a soothing transition between the seaside and downtown Riga.

– If you'd like to have a chicken coop there, I'll build you one.

– A generous offer.

– It will be the first and last work of my hands in Latvia. It will remain even when I no longer exist.

– You're being melodramatic…

I say Chekhov wrote in his notebook about a man who dug a well to save his soul. He did not want his life to vanish into eternity without a trace. Let the chicken coop be my well, since my own coop in Finland is already rotting away. Making something with their hands is what keeps Finnish men sane, or would do if such work still needed to be done.

– Now I understand why you use a feather for a bookmark, Vilma says.

– Are you familiar with chickens?

– I never saw my grandma's chickens. And I never learned to milk a cow.

Her grandmother had not wanted to stay in her house after her husband, a botany professor, was deported to Siberia. Vilma says her grandmother believed to the end that her husband would return. That belief kept her sane.

Anastasia moistens her front paw with her tongue and rubs the fur behind her ears. Vilma says the unqualified love of the creature melted her heart straightaway. Its presence consoled her in difficult times. She had already wanted a cat as a child, but her mother was allergic to cats.

Vilma says Anastasia is fifteen years old. Cats of her breed can live to be over twenty; they have not been spoiled by overbreeding, and they very rarely fall ill.

– The same is true of landrace chickens, I say.

– I got Anastasia as a replacement for my unborn child.

– What do you mean?

– A miscarriage.

Vilma traces the initials with her finger, and says the tablecloth is a cherished memento of her childhood. It recalls the enchantment of family coffee breaks and delicious pastries. The past comes alive when you find a locus for it.

Her grandfather was never heard from again. All that is left are photographs browning at the edges, letters, classic novels, a collection of pipes and some fine herbaria. Vilma has assembled these fragments into a portrait of the man, and a handsome one at that. Her grandfather seems closer to her than her own father, although she does not have a bad word to say about her father. Vilma believes that when she had spoken of wanting to learn chess as a child, her grandfather would have played with her if he had still been around.

– Your grandfather was not the architect of his own fortune, I say.

– Or was until that nocturnal knock on the door.

I say Finland just barely avoided being annexed to the Soviet family. If the peace-loving Soviet Union had succeeded in invading our country, Stalin would have had my parents executed, and I would never have existed. My father's Cross of Liberty would have wound up in a flea market among rusty fish lures. He could have been killed on the front any number of times, but he died as a melancholy old man. I inherited his fur coat with its Crimean sheep collar.

Vilma says that her school had competitions in dismantling and reassembling the trigger mechanism of a Kalashnikov. The teacher's right-hand trigger finger was missing, which Vilma found amusing. When the children practised shooting the gun, she stepped aside. As a result, she was refused entry into college.

I tell her that at an army competition I once aimed all ten shots at the edges of the target so that none of them hit the circles that gave points. I was rewarded for this feat with the order to empty all the latrines in the camp. At about the same time, a zealot friend of mine boasted that he had won a competition in air rifle shooting at a sauna evening held by the Helsinki representation of the GDR.

I later met a Finnish writer who said that she had been alone in her school yard in Viipuri when a fighter plane flew over. She could see the pilot's face as his machine gun sprayed the sand around her. As an adult, she thought perhaps the pilot had a child of his own and missed her on purpose. When travelling around Russia, she always hoped she would find that face so she could thank him.

– My chicken farm promoted the peaceful coexistence of Finland and Russia.

– Haha, how's that?

I photographed the East Karelian region which Finland had ceded to the Soviet Union after the war, finding something of the lost Finland of the past there, though in poor repair. In Uhtua, an old woman was selling eggs in front of her cottage. Having ascertained that the eggs were from landrace hens and fertilized by a rooster, I bought a score of eggs and placed them under a brooding hen when I got home.

The old woman radiated a very Russian kind of neighbourly love, which seemed to well up from pure goodness. She offered me a bed for the night and fed me brown bread, dried fish and cloudberries with whipped cream. In one corner of her cottage kitchen was a portrait of Karl Marx in a gilt frame. Why Marx as an icon? I asked. Who's Marx? she asked, and said she had bought the picture because the bearded fellow in it was the living image of her uncle, already long gone.

I tell Vilma that the eggs hatched and the chicks grew and blended into my flock without any problems. The internationalism of chickenkind is true, and poultry cluck the same Chicken Esperanto all over the world.

As the newcomers grew, however, my rooster realized that it had rivals and began to batter them, even though there was no deliberate evil in his behaviour. I had to wring the cockerels' necks and throw them in the pot. Peace was restored in the coop, and the chickens were all one family again, just like chess players according to the FIDE motto. In the chess world, too, there could only be one world champion at a time.

I still have questions I would like to discuss with Igors, but I do not expect to see him again. When my parents died, I also regretted questions never asked and words left unspoken.

– I know the feeling, Vilma said.

Igors has had a fabulous cosmopolitan journey. Before my trip, I thought I might write a feature story about him. Now that seems too little, and I would like to write a novel based on his chess career.

– Why the conditional?

– I probably won't have the time to finish it.

Previously, if a book was late through my own fault, I could ask the publisher for a postponement. There was no one to ask to postpone the deadline for my life.

– Rubbish! How do you know when the end will come? Fatalism is no use.

– That's what Igors said when complaining about the white-coats' predictions…

– You will write Igors's story. It's your apple tree.

– Planting an apple tree only takes a few hours.

– You won't need five hundred pages to tell the tale.

– Apple trees… They're in bloom in Jurmala. For a brief moment.

Vilma sits down next to me, strokes the back of my hand and says the best way to fight anxiety is to start something new. Even if your body is decaying, that does not have to mean that your mind will wither or your energy will run out.

– Indifference to living is the worst disease, she says.

– I won't say you're wrong…

– Once you get started, the story will find its natural course.

– You can't stop time by writing, I say.

– No, but you can tinge life with hope.

Vilma brings a bowl of olives to the table, plays with my hair and says that if Igors depended on success at chess for his livelihood, the obligation to win must have been a burden. Perhaps it had weakened his immune system, exposing him to cancer.

– Kitchen psychology, Vilma says.

– The same thought has occurred to me.

Since my own livelihood has always been secure, it is hard for me to identify with Igors. In my youth, pretending to be poor was a pose. Money is only money, as long as you have enough of it. Igors, too, used to have plenty. Now he is spending his nights sitting in his hermitage, watching the movements of a long-eared hare from the window and earning five euros an hour for doing nothing.

I add that I have wondered how Igors's life would have turned out if, instead of chess, he had dedicated himself to medicine, which he had studied for six years. Perhaps he would have developed a cancer drug that prolonged and eased the lives of millions of people. But God had ignited in him the spark of chess, and this had enabled him to make his home anywhere in the world. He even seemed at home in his shack, and never grumbled about it or his guard job. As Ajgul said, he had made a virtue of necessity.

According to Igors, the game of chess as such does not lead to anything, but it determined his life's path. He appreciated his Soviet-era privilege of being able to travel where he wished. He had met his previous wife at a chess tournament in Riga, and his current one when travelling to a tournament in Paris.

– Chess also brought us together, I sigh and put my arms around Vilma.

– We could have met in Paris, too, Vilma said.

– Perhaps at the basin in the Jardin du Luxembourg, when you were playing chess, I said.

– What were you doing there?

– Photographing ducklings jumping on and off sailboats in the basin.

Vilma says she once met a writer who had moved from Leningrad to Riga. He told her that many Russian intellectuals had remained homeless in their new home country. They were attached to their national roots, language, home region and friends, and this attachment followed them all their lives, regardless of where fate hurled them. They felt that they lost a part of their personality when speaking in a foreign language, since their words lacked nuance and wit. Russian chess players also tended to make poor immigrants. Life always seemed better somewhere else.

I had met plenty of American Finns in Minnesota. According to them, third-generation immigrants wished to remember what the second generation had forgotten. In the village of Finland, I watched a competition in which the participating teams took turns pushing an outdoor toilet on the ice of a frozen lake. Perhaps this event was linked to the need to remember.

– It didn't correspond to my idea of the American Dream.

– America, too, is many things, Vilma said.

Igors had gone out into the world of his own free will, if such a thing exists. He was like Aki Kaurismäki, the film director, who said his home was where his hat was. As far as I know, Aki never wore a hat.

Igors had taught and played chess in many different countries, but had never attached any larger-than-life meaning to it. In this respect, he was like a priest without faith. If he had accepted that he had passed his prime in competitive chess and was facing an inevitable decline, he could have retired elegantly as a grandmaster.

– If he had, Vilma sniffs.

Vilma says she has known writers and filmmakers whose narrative urge and skill had withered. Some of them found it hard to accept this, and whinged at their uncomprehending family and friends. History also knew of rulers and business leaders who did not have the sense to hang up their gloves in time. Their procrastination had resulted in much trouble and gnashing of teeth.

On the other hand, Sunday writers and painters can go on as long as they can hold a pencil or a paintbrush, as far as Vilma is concerned. The same goes for chess amateurs, since playing brings them pleasure to the very end.

I say I no longer have any manuscripts in my desk drawer. My books document a vanishing Finland. At the same time, they are an integral part of my life, which is also about to vanish. The documentary character of my books was a by-product that I never thought about when writing them. My incentive consisted of curiosity and the creative urge that my disease is now gnawing at.

My books will be my monument, since I do not desire one in stone. I need not fear that my notable achievements at the bank will be overlooked, for there were none. All that will be left of the quarter-century of my gradually declining career is a pair of silver cufflinks that I never once used.

My book of Berlin photographs is about to go into print. Previously, I always had the idea for my next book clear in my mind. No such topic has materialized this time around.

– But now a wonderful topic has chosen you and is waiting on a silver platter, Vilma says. Igors's life has all the makings of a great story. As told by you or a character like you, it will provide a fascinating double exposure of the soul of chess and approaching death, showing how hard it is to let go.

According to Vilma, world literature has a gap in it the size of a good chess novel. Like football, chess is a universal and timeless game. They have much in common: a football coach plays chess with his team of chessmen. Both disciplines bring joy to their adepts, and it is irrelevant to ask whether either of them produces any material good for humankind.

She says a story can express the conflicting and unpredictable nature of emotions, objectives and actions. Americans love success stories, whereas Russians often write about failure. Which category Igors's story falls under is an interesting question.

– The topic fascinates you. When you are writing, you live in an eternal present. No disease can take that away.

– All right then, what name shall we give the child?

– *Chess Is Only a Game*, Vilma says.

– Uh...um.

– The title raises the question whether it really is just a game.

– It is for some, but not for others, I say.

– Exactly, Vilma says. You've already gained Igors's trust. In a literary sense, you should keep your distance and avoid making it either a denunciation or a plea of innocence. You can't x-ray a human soul, but you can sense its subtleties, and the cracks in it, beyond words, gestures and expressions. Every one of us has something to hide. There's plenty of depth in the themes of cheating and shame.

Why do we cheat and act immorally? According to Vilma, we are particularly good at deluding ourselves. We give ourselves up to the very actions we despise. Most people have a clear understanding of right and wrong, but that is no help. In practice, it is hard to live by our convictions. We are imperfect, and absolute honesty is impossible. And chess is certainly no enclave of innocence.

I pick an olive from the bowl and say that I once exchanged Finnish marks for rubles at the black-market rate in Leningrad. I trusted that heaven is high and the emperor far away. I knew I was doing wrong, but silenced the voice of conscience.

The money dealer said he was honest in his dealings, which he considered a mark of immaturity. A colleague of his would place old lottery tickets under a banknote. In their vodka-induced stupor, tourists rarely checked the whole pile. His colleague thought this served the tourists right. I agreed with him.

I had a scare when a *militsiya* officer in a peaked cap appeared on the scene halfway through our transaction. The dealer offered him a cigarette and said, "Don't be frightened, Sergei is a friend." Once again, friendship showed its power.

Anastasia rubs herself against my leg. I stroke her intently and tell Vilma about the owner of a Sicilian *trattoria* who roasted cats and served them to his guests as hares. Perhaps he was trying to pay off his debts. When the truth came out, he no longer wished to remain in his home town. He sold the trattoria, which was renamed the Real Hares Restaurant.

Igors has changed his name to shield his family from his shame. He has adopted Ajgul's surname and picked a first name from Arabic, which he learned as a child. He now calls himself Isa Kasimi. Isa means 'prophet' or 'Jesus'; not that he thinks of himself as Jesus. I once saw a T-shirt that read *Jesus is coming* on the front and *Jesus is going* on the back. The man who wore it did not look like a megalomaniac, either.

Vilma says she thinks Igors's act was an error that he had perhaps already committed mentally before the tournament. Perhaps he was seeking punishment, like Raskolnikov in Dostoevsky's novel.

Igors is one of us. As Vilma puts it, it is always other people who are evil and deceitful. We all have our defects, and we can all be crushed by our weaknesses. We need and love scapegoats, to be able to beat our breasts: thank God we are not unworthy like those people. Who can afford to cast the first stone at Igors?

When Igors betrayed his principles, he caused a fracture with which he must live. Readers will find analogies with their own lives in his situation.

Vilma says that when reading a novel or watching a film, she is moved if it conveys the feeling of a solution, of beauty, joy or sorrow with which readers or viewers can identify and after which they are no longer the same. Sometimes they may recall a forgotten experience of their own. These are the kind of moments she would like to put in her own films.

Two sick men sit in a shack on a building site in the midst of a waste land. They discuss chess, choices, life and death; they sip tea and reminisce about their childhood.

– The story has all the ingredients needed for a feature film, Vilma says.

– Chance brought me to this forecourt of heaven with your cigarette case in my pocket. That could also be a film scene.

– But is chance really chance?

Vilma says that Kieslowski's film *Blind Chance* showed the director's views on the impossibility of making rational choices in a world where an apparently trivial coincidence can derail one's whole life. The protagonist runs to catch a train at the station. Depending on whether or not he is in time, his life can take three different directions: he will focus either on furthering his own career, exposing injustices or pursuing happiness.

When photographing the Islamic cemetery in Helsinki, I met a Tatar carpet merchant visiting his grandfather's grave. He told me his grandfather had left his home in the bend of the River Volga and taken a train to St Petersburg. He had fallen asleep on the train, only waking up when it pulled into the station in Helsinki. He liked the town and stayed. He later became a mainstay of *Altin Ordan* ('The Golden Horde'), the Turkic Tatars' football club in Helsinki.

My train had passed Zolitūde and I had woken up at Tornakalnus station. Because I had dozed off, Vilma and I happened to be sitting face to face. If Igors had not been hospitalized, I would be sitting in his shack now. Perhaps fate is offering me a new direction.

The Queen's Gambit also features random encounters that Vilma considers credible and that help Beth succeed. Beth has the good sense not to shut the door on them, which is the whole point.

Vilma says that chess gurus cannot find fault with anything in *The Queen's Gambit*. On the other hand, the series also impresses viewers who do not have the slightest notion of what chess is about. It manages to strike a balance between mystery and narrative clarity. I should write my novel in the same spirit.

Vilma thinks that Igors's career and the world of chess could provide a cover story and a bridge to the most important themes. Death is a topic that no one can elude.

– At the same time you can tell the story of your escape to Riga – explain it to yourself, too.

– Fear of death is a tough subject, I say.

– It only has one cure, Vilma says.

– And what's that, if I may ask?

– Not to fear it or demonize it.

– You're joking.

– Not at all.

Vilma thinks we must accept the end and face it with tenderness, like Bergman did in his films. Igors seems to understand this and to show himself mercy.

The Italian poet Cesare Pavese wrote: "It is good to be alive because living is beginning, always, every moment". Vilma says she has framed that line and pinned it to the wall.

– Think about that, Matti dear.

– A touching thought, I say with a tremor in my voice, and caress her neck.

She apologizes for her didactic tone, but she is a teacher, and narration is a crucial part of her profession. One of her students told Vilma she speaks like a priest in Sunday school. Startled, she urged her students to adopt a critical attitude to her sermons: some things can be taught, but not the truth, which you have to experience for yourself.

– All the same, it's possible to learn something from a work of art, Vilma says.

– Marx said the social tendency in art should not stick out like a spring from a sofa, I say.

– Many of his followers don't understand this, Vilma says.

– The egg isn't always smarter than the chicken.

– By the way, would you like another glass of Chianti? Vilma asks, leaning her hand on my shoulder and kissing my cheek.

She fills our glasses and says she is keeping an eye on advertisements of old houses for sale in Jurmala. One has to be prepared to renovate, since the prices of new houses have gone through the roof. One may also have to film commercials, even though one would prefer not to.

– I can build you a chicken coop from waste materials, I say.

– Will it have a gable roof?

– Yes. Or a lean-to roof.

– How will you decide which?

– Depends on the style of your house. Will you come to the book launch?

– For sure. A toast to Igors's story!

My mobile phone beeps: a text message. Instead of reading it, I open the Ryanair website, key in my code and cancel my booking for tomorrow's flight.

I show Vilma the photo on my phone showing me in a Russian platform attendant's uniform complete with peaked cap. The train stopped at the station twice a day. I caught the evening service, which had something of the atmosphere of the train to Jurmala or the trains of my childhood.

– The attendant agreed to lend me his uniform for a bottle of vodka.

– A paltry price for fulfilling a childhood dream, Vilma says.

– The journey continues…

I take the folding birchwood chessboard from the bookshelf, set up the pieces, hide a white pawn in one hand and a black pawn in the other, and give Vilma an inviting look.

– Vilma dear, let's play!

JUHANI SEPPOVAARA
(b. 1947) is a Finnish writer
and photographer with over
20 published works to his
credit. He previously worked
for a quarter of a century as
an economist at the Bank of
Finland and, at the same time,
as an organic chicken farmer.
He is now living in Berlin.